D0616729

The SEARCH *for the* HOMESTEAD TREASURE

THE
Search
FOR THE
HOMESTEAD
TREASURE

ANN TREACY

University of Minnesota Press

Minneapolis · London

Published by the University of Minnesota Press
111 Third Avenue South, Suite 290
Minneapolis, MN 55401–2520
http://www.upress.umn.edu

ISBN 978-0-8166-9956-8 (hc)
ISBN 978-1-5179-0171-4 (pb)
A Cataloging-in-Publication record for this book is available from the Library of Congress.

Design and production by Mighty Media, Inc.
Interior and text design by Chris Long

Printed in the United States of America on acid-free paper

The University of Minnesota is an equal-opportunity educator and employer.

22 21 20 19 18 17 16   10 9 8 7 6 5 4 3 2 1

For Annie Koehnen
1884–1893

The best place to find a helping hand
is at the end of your own arm.
—Swedish proverb

All truths are easy to understand once they are
discovered; the point is to discover them.
—Galileo Galilei

Goodhue County, Minnesota
6 July 1865

Cora awoke hearing blackbirds bark, cicadas buzz, and Mother shifting about in the cabin. She was tempted to open her eyes, but Cora knew if she appeared to be sleeping, Mother might allow her to stay in bed longer. The trick was to relax her face because if she squeezed her eyes, Mother would know she was playing possum.

The glow through her eyelids told her that the sun was already well up. She smelled sour soot as the sun warmed the roof and stovepipe. Waves of pungent ammonia reminded her that the washtub was filled with baby linens that could not wait another day for washing. That alone was a good reason to stay in bed, because now that she was thirteen years old, Cora had to help with the washings.

But there were reasons to get up. The pitcher of milk would have clotted overnight on the sideboard, making it perfect for griddlecakes or bread.

Mother's shadow came close and blocked the bright sun illuminating Cora's eyelids.

"Min bästa flicka . . . My best girl, you look like a princess but sleep like a field mouse." Mother lingered longer than usual at her bedside. She gently cupped Cora's forehead with her rough hand. The hand felt hot and moist like steamy linen being pressed.

Then Cora heard long skirts sweep the floorboards as Mother moved toward Jacob's crib. She peeked enough to see Mother feel the baby's face, then her own, then walk out the cabin door. Cora settled into her feather tick. She felt successful at her game if she was still pretending to be asleep when Mother pumped water for morning coffee. But Mother didn't take the teakettle with her this morning. Cora looked straight out the open door and saw Mother weakly working the pump handle. When a trickle began, Mother reached for a handful of water and poured it down the open neck of her long nightdress.

Cora heard the cabin door close, and then the bed ropes creaked. Mother was going back to bed! Was she playing possum, too? Usually Mother got up hours before the children to hoe the rapidly growing vegetables. Cora crept out of bed and spider-walked her fingers up Mother's arm to surprise her.

"Good morning."

"God morgon, dotter."

Cora understood Swedish but always answered in English. "Aren't you getting up?"

"I'll just lie here a minute. It must be the heat." Mother's smile did not reach her blue eyes. Her face looked lined and old.

It was odd to be up and see Mother in bed. She was never sick. "I'll haul the water today," Cora offered. "And feed the chickens. I can be so quiet Jacob won't wake up."

When Cora came in from her chores, Mother's face glistened like summer butter. Cora had never heard such raspy breathing. She stood still and listened. Mother began shaking in the bed and mumbling. *"Dotter,"* Mother whispered, *"min vacker lilla dotter."* My beautiful little daughter.

What was happening? Mother seemed as sick as some
of the animals Cora had seen die. Except Mother was young
and healthy. She was Anna Gunnarsson; she had survived the
voyage from Sweden. Mother was beautiful. Father had been
young when he died, but the war had killed him. Cora went
to the bed and shook Mother's wrist.

Mother's hand fluttered to her heart. "I am so sick. I need
you to listen about the baby. You must take Jacob to Mrs.
Perry. Now."

"It's too far." Cora was frightened by the way Mother
gasped for air. She had never seen anyone like this before.
Mother struggled to breathe as if she had swallowed thick
molasses.

"You have to." Mother clutched at Cora's arm. "But first,
you must get something from the wood box."

"*Mor,* let me bring you water instead."

"Go to the wood box. Do it now, *dotter.*"

Cora backed toward the box by the hearth.

Mother coughed deep in her chest. "Dig out the oil
cloth . . . at the bottom . . . under the logs."

Cora struggled to lift a heavy, wrapped bundle that felt
like a lead baby. "Bring it here," Mother choked. She placed
her hands around the girl's arms, sealing the parcel in them.
"This is yours now. Put it somewhere safe. With your pa
dead, it's all you have for your life."

Mother's hands swam across the coverlet, and she began
to mumble as if Cora weren't there. "Carl, I should have told
you I brought a dowry. I've been so upset since you died . . .
should never . . . kept secret . . . from my husband. If you had
known, we could have had a better place, a place closer to
town. Closer to a doctor . . ."

Cora hid the awkward bundle in the safest place she
knew. When she returned Mother was still talking to Father,
but he was dead. Tears brimmed in Cora's eyes as she patted
cold water on her mother's burning face. Baby Jacob stirred
in his bed. "Wake up, *Mor.*" Then louder: "Wake up."

Mother gasped. Without opening her eyes she whispered,

"The dowry will take you and baby Jacob far. Start now, go to the Perrys, *min söta flicka.*" Mother did not speak another word.

What was happening, and so quickly? Cora did not go directly to the Perry farm. For the first time in her life she disobeyed. Even with Jacob and Mother near her in their beds, she couldn't remember a time when she felt so alone. She curled up in the rocker with her familiar blue diary and took comfort in writing an entry.

6 July 1865
Mother is sick. Not even Father was this sick. She told me to take Jacob to the Perrys. Her last words were about a dowry, which I hid safely in my doll's house. Jacob is starting to cry. I am afraid to disobey her, but I am also afraid to leave her alone.

Baby Jacob screamed. Cora put down her pencil and dipped the corner of a clean pillow linen in boiled sugar water for him to suck. Rocking the baby, she bent over her mother, but the ashen woman no longer responded, not even when Cora bounced the oak bed frame with her knee.

Cora's legs wobbled. Her own throat began to burn and she felt her forehead with the back of her hand. The image of Mother doing the same flashed in her mind. It was nothing, only the heat of the day. She put down the few belongings she had gathered for Jacob and walked out of the farmhouse with nothing but her brother.

CHAPTER

Goodhue County, Minnesota
February 1903

"Way over there," Pa pointed across an empty expanse of frozen field, "is where they found Cora and me."
Fourteen-year-old Martin Gunnarsson listened as his father told the story of being found in a field, like Moses in the bulrushes. Despite his anger at having to leave Stillwater and his friends, Martin listened carefully. He only knew bits about his father's childhood, as Pa didn't speak of it much. In the front wagon seat Ma was silent as always, but so was Aunt Ida, which was rare.

Pa went on. "Cora wasn't dead, not yet, of the diphtheria. She must have lain there most of a day, face up to the sun; they say she was scorched pretty bad. Not me though. She covered me with her apron."

Pa lightly flipped the reins over the plodding horses' backs. "It was summer; I imagine crops were tall then. 'Course I was just a baby and don't remember. They say it was my wailing on toward sundown that brought the dogs."

Their wagon was so heavily laden with household goods

that it rode more smoothly than usual. In the back of the wagon bed, seven-year-old Lilly had to sit almost in Martin's lap. She played with a sack of clothespin dolls. As Pa talked she hummed and whispered. She dropped clothespins onto the wagon floor as she acted out the story of how first his mother, then his sister had died of diphtheria.

Lilly looked up from her dolls. "Was Cora beautiful, Pa?"

"Dang it," Martin swore softly. Every time Lilly turned to speak, she bumped his whittling arm. She stuck her tongue out at him. A wagon was no place to do fine work, so for an hour he had just cut notches into a pin, like a gunslinger cut notches in his revolver handle.

"I don't know, little Lilly," Pa called back. "I was too young to remember her, and she was years older. I've never seen a likeness of her, but the Perrys always did say she had beautiful yellow hair. Maybe like yours."

"And the gold? Tell about the gold and riches," Lilly said.

Martin pushed Lilly's skirt off his pants leg. He'd heard the lost riches story before, mostly because Pa didn't have anything *real* to tell about his family. Pa's father died in the states' war, and his mother died when he was a baby. The Perrys were nice neighbors to raise him, but they knew little about the Gunnarsson family's background. Martin sometimes wondered if Pa still had relatives in Sweden they knew nothing about.

Pa shook his head. "That was just a rumor started by Mrs. Perry. I guess she was about my mother's only lady friend. The Perrys raised me on the very next homestead. Sometimes they would rent out my parents' place to croppers, but as far as I know, in over thirty years nobody has found anything there but hard work."

Aunt Ida snorted. She was Ma's aunt, old, thin, and white-haired. But she was also wiry and spry and rarely failed to speak her mind. "These farms are hard living, all right. Hard on horses and hell on women."

That hard work would fall to him. Martin missed home. Not the bad times since his brother Dan had died, but the good things like his friends Stan and Chet and the firehouse. He loved polishing lights on the rig and visiting the huge horses that pulled the water wagon. He would go back. He would give Pa a year. Get the first crop in and paying. By then he'd be fifteen. Lots of fifteen-year-olds lived away and worked.

Martin stretched his collar. Ma had laid out Sunday clothes today for their arrival. Sunday clothes under winter coats were uncomfortable enough, but the collar and socks weren't even his. Poverty, Martin thought, was wearing your dead brother's clothes.

Lilly attempted to stand in order to rearrange her woolen petticoats. "Are we almost there, Pa?"

"As the crow flies, it's not far. But by road we have to go the long way around. Not a terrible lot has changed out here, except that most of these old places are being bought up."

Dunes of gray snow sagged in the brown fields. Martin couldn't imagine this bleak, frozen countryside was desirable to anyone. Yet Pa looked the happiest he had in months, leaning forward on the wagon bench to see past Aunt Ida. "It's the chance of a lifetime, Martha. Of course, we have to make the taxes, or the bank will get our place. I'm lucky Robert Perry offered the homestead back to me."

Our place. Martin knew that during the war Pa's parents had started a homestead on 160 acres. But they couldn't have gotten much built up before they both died. Martin wished Pa had let the bank have it.

Pa whistled and looked across the wagon seat at Ma. Ma, who used to excite so easily, rarely spoke since Dan died. She didn't smile and hadn't commented on leaving her home. She just reached into her coat pocket and doctored herself with a spoonful of cough tonic, then slowly said, "If you say so, Jacob."

They heard the jangle of approaching teams beyond a rise in the road ahead. All five fell silent in anticipation. Cresting the hill were several dozen brightly painted wagons, like an approaching carnival caravan.

"What's ahead, Pa?" Martin called.

Lilly turned and knelt to see over the side of the wagon. She studied the approaching procession of dark-skinned people in various odd wagons. "Who are they?"

Aunt Ida clasped her hands to her bony chest and gasped as Pa answered, "Gypsies."

As fast as a cow kicks, old Aunt Ida was on her feet. "Heathen Egyptians," she spat. "They rob people blind and disappear in the night." She pushed up her black parasol and tilted it toward the oncoming wagons. "I won't be able to sleep tonight if they cast their eye on me."

Lilly ducked her head, trying to hide behind the wagon's side. But curiosity soon brought her head slowly up again like a sunflower following the sun.

In Stillwater, Martin had been accustomed to seeing Indians, and in his lifetime he had seen three men with black skin. But these people were different, and he couldn't help but stare as their odd wagons passed Pa's plodding team. For once Lilly didn't fidget but watched the procession of people in loose-fitting clothes who appeared to come from another world.

Aunt Ida complained about the bad omen of crossing paths with Gypsies on the trip to their new home. But Pa, who usually tried to console Aunt Ida, was busy appraising each passing horse with the practiced eye of a lumber camp farrier. Pa knew horses. It was his job to shoe them and do general doctoring of sprains and colic. For all their large size, workhorses had touchy constitutions.

Martin hadn't seen such a parade of horseflesh since the county fair. He studied the people, too, although most of the Gypsies kept their eyes averted. A girl and boy skipped along the roadside playing with two dogs. A woman held a baby on her lap, face forward, to be entertained by the sights.

Just people. With children just like us. Their children even look happy, the way we used to be, Martin thought.

Suddenly Lilly pulled a quilt over her head to protect her

open satchel of doll clothes from the road dust. She peered up at Martin. "Will they scalp us?"

"Silly Lilly," Martin said. "Nobody gets scalped anymore. It's 1903."

"Probably do worse," Aunt Ida snorted from the squeaky spring seat. Her thin frame rocked as she hid behind the parasol. "Sneak up in the night, rob you, slit your throat, and disappear faster than cream in an orphanage."

Ma rode in silence, but not because she cared about the passing horses as Pa did. Ever since Dan was whisked away like a sheet from a bed, Ma didn't laugh or even manage to prop up her side of a conversation. Dan had been the oldest, Lilly's preferred brother, and the only one of the children able to cajole Aunt Ida into making his favorite foods or Ma into changing her rules.

The wagon lurched on toward a new, lonely life. Martin took out his grief and examined it as if it were a thing to be held. No, it was no longer the worst numbing grief, but it was still a constant sense of loss. He thought about climbing the St. Croix River cliffs just two days ago with his friends. Right now he missed them almost more than Dan. He felt like cargo being hauled to a farm, and farming had never interested him.

Just before dark Pa turned the horses and wagon onto a road that shrank to a narrow, overgrown trail. When the wagon finally stopped in a small clearing, Pa grinned more broadly than Martin had ever seen.

"My boyhood home," Pa said happily. "Well, I was born here anyway."

Martin stood to look. There was an old barn and a small house. Beyond, in the evening darkness, he made out several former structures melting into the earth from disrepair. Even though for a year Martin had filled the conversations left empty by Ma's silence, he couldn't think of one thing to say now to Pa. He opened his mouth but nothing came out.

Even Aunt Ida was silent. She just patted Ma's hand.

Lilly had busied herself with packing up her dolls. "Are we there?" She pulled herself up against the wagon sides. "Where are we?"

The gloom of the cold February day was changing to blackness. At home, street lamps would be lit by now. Awkwardly, as if he had never done it before, Martin climbed out of the wagon in his Sunday clothes and stood in the bleak yard. No fabled fortune had helped Pa's family forty years ago, and it wouldn't help his family now.

A terrible longing settled over him. He had known deep yearnings since the accident—the "if onlys" and bargaining-with-God feelings of wishing his brother back to life. The difference was that they could undo this move. This regret was reversible, at least for him. He would make sure of it.

CHAPTER

"Ain't those perty town shoes," Dale Barker whispered as Martin stepped into the aisle.

Miss Abrams had asked, "Martin, the new boy, how many stars are on the American flag?" Although he answered correctly, she reminded him to "always stand to recite."

Martin unclenched his teeth and stood and repeated, "Forty-five." After attending the one-room school for several weeks, he had abandoned hope that Miss Abrams would ever address him without adding "new boy" to his name. His Stillwater teacher, Mrs. Walters, was smart and fun. Here the boys joked that Miss Abrams had been a passenger on the *Santa Maria.*

To make matters worse, with Pa gone to work at the lumber camps, Martin had no horse. He missed Finn and Marshall, his father's workhorses, and also the light team they had owned before Dan's accident. If they still had them, he could ride to school like the other boys. Martin ate lunch alone and walked home alone. Since they had no way to get to town, their food supply had dwindled, and he had nothing but boiled potatoes and hardtack in his lunch pail.

On a typically cold but sunny morning in late March, Miss Abrams finally rang the lunch bell. As usual, the boys scrambled out to eat where their horses were hitched. Frank

Barker, Dale's brother, punched Martin from behind and said, "Think you're smart knowing all the answers, city boy?"

Martin wanted to hit him back, but it was better not to call attention to himself. He pretended to go to the privy, then slipped away and made for the deep lake at the back of the Perrys' side forty.

Hang school. He would spend the day fishing and damn the consequences. Who would find out anyway? Or care?

In his pocket he carried a cork with a hook stuck in it and line wrapped around, just as he and his friends had done in Stillwater. Near the rock dump at the edge of the field, he stopped to pry up several large stones. He scoured the exposed earth until he found pale grub worms, their little legs working, some moist fat slugs, and one june bug. Years of living with Aunt Ida had convinced him that june bugs brought good luck. Whenever a june bug made its way inside she'd say, "You daresn't kill one," and then ceremoniously sweep it out to the garden. Martin grabbed the hard-shelled beetle that was the size of a pecan and thrust the spoils into his jacket pocket.

At the lake he lanced the wiggly june bug onto his hook with the same care his mother took threading a needle. Next he attached the line to a stick. Deeper water was best for fishing, and the only way to get out over it was to carefully walk along the trunk of an oak that had fallen into the lake. He settled against the largest branch, which pointed straight up from the horizontal trunk, and lowered the madly dancing june bug into the water.

It didn't take long to get results. Waving the plump insect over fish was like calling field hands to a threshers' breakfast. Martin stood half upright against the branch, working the line, letting it play. He stared hard at the water, waiting for his eyes to adjust to the sun's reflection so he could see underneath the surface.

A cloud passing screened the sun's glare. He saw two things move at the same time: a large gray fish and black grass waving farther out under the trunk in deeper water. He trained his gaze on the spot while his hands wrapped the line several times around a branch. He spider-walked his way farther up the sloping tree trunk until he looked directly down at the curious, undulating black mass.

Martin firmly grabbed two branches and lowered his face close to the water's cold surface. He saw an arm and hand at the same instant that he recognized it was hair, not grass, floating deep beneath the surface of the lake.

Human hair. There was a body down there. *A dead body.* His grip slipped. One foot shot down for support but plunged into the water. He clambered back up, scraping his hands and ripping his jacket sleeve as he scratched and hugged the tree trunk.

He considered what to do. Town was miles away. He could go and tell Mr. Perry. But Pa said Mr. Perry's health was ailing, and what could Mr. Perry do anyway? Martin let go with one hand and sculled the water in an effort to clearly see the face.

The head faced downward so he couldn't make out features. He hadn't heard anyone was missing, but his family had no way to get to town.

Sooner or later, someone had to pull out the body. Martin figured it might as well be him. Was there even a county sheriff here—or any law? He yanked off his shoes and jacket, tied them in a tight bundle using the sleeves, then hurled it to shore. With one hand he swung out and lowered his legs half into the water. He caught his breath with the initial cold shock, released the branch, and let himself drop the rest of the way.

The full jolt of the icy water petrified his muscles. Martin dragged himself to the surface to refill his lungs, then dove downward with his arms. He could see well underwater. Back home, he, Chet, and Stan had often thrown things to the bottom of the St. Croix River, then raced each other to retrieve them.

He explored the silent reedy bottom until he came face-to-face with the large, unblinking brown eyes of a boy who appeared to have several sticks in his mouth. Martin knew people sometimes died with their eyes open. He knew firsthand. Probably that was the case in drowning, too. He grabbed one of the corpse's elbows.

Bubbles spewed from the dead boy's mouth just as an arm released a submerged branch and swung toward Martin.

What! Martin heard himself gasp despite being underwater.

The dislodged body grabbed at him. Martin lurched back and fought upward. Cold swallowed water burned down his core. He sucked air and swam to the safety of the fallen tree's branches. Then he twisted around.

A head bobbed up. Teeth flashed in the sun. Arms windmilled. The head went under.

Martin spat icy water and hooked an arm into the branch to rest from the shock.

Again the head churned to the surface. "Ga!"

Why the hell would a person be play-drowning out—

The flying arms brought the boy up, farther out this time. Look at him. How'd he know I'd come along anyway?

Thrashing. A weak "Help."

Fool me once. He's half fish to hold his breath underwater so long.

Twenty feet away the churning slowed.

Maybe he wasn't fooling now. Martin pushed off the tree trunk, sliced across the water, and grabbed a fistful of hair. With one hand he dragged the impostor back to the tree.

"Hey!" He pulled the face up by the fistful of hair.

Still the boy played dead.

"Cut it out!" Martin's toes found an underwater branch for support, freeing his other hand. "You." He slapped the boy's face.

Nothing.

"Knock it off!" With energy fueled by the Barkers' teasing and anger over losing his friends, home, and brother all merging into hatred, he pulled back and punched the boy. Hot tears mixed with icy water on Martin's cheeks. He clutched a fistful of shirt. "Hey! What were you doing?"

The boy's head lolled. He gagged, opened his eyes, closed them, and vomited.

"You crazy?" Martin coughed and shivered. The false spring sunshine failed to warm him as he pulled up on the tree.

The boy didn't follow. His skin had been brown but now it looked gray. Both of his hands were white from clutching branches. Martin heaved him up and saw he wore only a shirt and woolen underwear, cut off at the knees. "I thought you were dead under there."

The boy lay across the trunk, his mouth still dripping water. He appeared shorter than Martin but it was hard to tell with him rolled over the log. He was bigger around, and even his back seemed pudgy, all cinched in by the top of his underwear. He turned his head. "I am thankful you."

"What?"

"I am thankful you. I am Samson. Sam."

Water dripped from the boy's several chins. He had long hair, so black it looked blue. Martin had never known anyone named Samson and blurted, "Like in the Bible?"

Samson shrugged. "Who are you?"

"Martin Gunnarsson. Who are you? I haven't seen you at school."

"I don't go." The boy looked away. "We are new here."

Martin jerked a thumb at the lake. "What were you doing down there?"

"Practicing my magic." Samson sat up and started crawling down the tree toward shore. He grabbed a hidden bundle of clothes and dressed as quickly as frozen hands allowed. "It is an Indian trick. I climb down the branches. I stay under by breathing through reeds. I can't swim. I'm sorry I scare you."

"I'm sorry I hit you." At least the boy had dry pants to put on. Martin was in a fine fix: he was freezing, his clothes were soaked, and he couldn't return home until school was out. "Where do you live?"

The boy pointed across the lake. "Over there in the meadow."

Martin had passed the meadow where traveling preachers held revival meetings. There were no homes there. The boy was pulling on bright pants and an odd jacket. Instead of a belt he tied a sash at his waist. All at once Martin knew. *Gypsy.*

Samson motioned. "Come with me. Dry your clothes."

Trembling, Martin crossed his dripping arms. His jaw hurt from shivering uncontrollably. The homestead was much farther away than the meadow.

His delay caused the boy to look hurt. "I go now."

Martin blew on his hands. He thought of the hook and line far out on the tree but was too stiff to climb out and retrieve them. Was it possible to die from being this cold and wet? He grabbed his city shoes and followed Samson.

Martin and Sam hurried out of the dark forest into the clearing. Caravans of various colors and styles were scattered around the meadow. Martin couldn't take his eyes off the well-groomed horses. He was so fascinated by his surroundings that he forgot to be afraid of this forbidden place. Aunt Ida would boil him in the laundry cauldron if she knew where he was.

At first he didn't notice that Samson was walking him around the camp, not through it.

Samson knocked on the door of a green and orange wagon and motioned Martin to follow him inside. Martin had anticipated darkness, but the wagon was parked to catch the sun through its one generous window. Samson rummaged in a drawer. Handing clothes to Martin he stepped back through the wagon's door. "Put these on and throw your clothes out to me."

Left alone, Martin studied the cozy traveling home. Everything was, as Aunt Ida would say, "spit spot," although some things were smaller than Martin considered usual, like the pallet beds. The room was uncluttered; he'd seen many things stored on the ground under the wagon.

He changed into pants that were huge and a shirt that bloused generously. As he lifted his head from tucking in the shirt, he realized someone had been watching through a slat in the shutter. He heard a commotion outdoors.

Samson was arguing with a beautiful girl. Their language was odd but that they were disagreeing was unmistakable. He stopped yelling and gestured to the girl when Martin approached. "This is Ruby, my cousin. We live here with our grandmother."

Martin was surprised that Ruby had green eyes. Her hair was less dark than her cousin's, and she was taller. She wore a loosely gathered skirt and emerald blouse that was not tucked in. Over both was knotted a crimson sash. Martin felt himself redden as he wondered what Gypsy women wore under their clothes. She looked round and soft, not hard and tight like corseted women.

"Why did you bring *him* here?" she asked in English but added something for emphasis in words Martin couldn't understand. One word sounded like *gorgeous.*

Samson didn't answer her and motioned Martin to follow. As Samson led him through the camp, Martin felt the prick of eyes on him. A black wire was stretched between trees at the forest's edge. There the boy hung Martin's clothes to dry. "They dry faster near fire, but then you smell of smoke and people ask why no school today."

The boys sat on a bench away from the collection of wagons.

"My *baba*—I think you say 'grandmother'—will be back soon," Samson said, kicking at the dirt. "I should not have brought you here."

"Why not?"

"My people don't like it. We live among the *gorgios,* but we don't bring outsiders into camp. We are Roma people. You call us Gypsies. We keep to ourselves."

Martin remembered Aunt Ida referring to Gypsies as heathen Egyptians. "Are you people Egyptian?"

Samson shook his head. "We got that name long ago. Folks thought we started out in Egypt."

"What does *gorgeous* mean?"

"*Gorgios*. Non-Gypsies. Like you."

"Where is your grandmother?"

"In town. For Gypsies, men do the work with horses and such, but women earn the money. Grandmother sells her sewing and charms and also tells fortunes."

"Fortunes? Like reading palms?"

Samson nodded. "Like that. She does the palms because people expect it, but Grandmother has the sight."

"The what?" Martin asked.

"Second sight. She just knows about people. All people. Always."

Martin couldn't believe he was in the midst of a true Gypsy encampment, discussing soothsayers. Doubt must have shown on his face because Samson continued.

"You don't believe." Samson searched for words with his hands. "I want choose a different life. These are my people, but I don't fit here. Everywhere we go I study people. You have one place, go to school, have real home. My life? I am called thief."

Martin thought of Aunt Ida and was embarrassed. "Let me tell you—living on a farm isn't that great. We just moved here from the town I grew up in. My parents are broke." He held his hands flat and shook them. "No money." He didn't mention Dan and the fancy funeral. "They spent everything trying to get back the homestead my pa was born on. So now there's no money to even buy me a horse."

"Where do you want live?"

"I want to go back home, to Stillwater. I'm counting on it."

"We live always on other people's property. We're chased out and made fun of. I would like farm. To me, land is many hope." He looked uncertain about what he'd said, then tried again. "Land is hopes." Samson broke off a fat blade of grass, clasped it between his thumbs, and placed his mouth over his hands. Blowing produced a loud, shrill call, which was immediately answered by a blackbird, then two. If he blew twice, the birds responded twice; if he blasted once, they answered with one long call.

"That's amazing," Martin said.

"Just one of my tricks." The boy beamed. "I love magic."

No longer getting an answer, the large birds called more loudly from the tall pines behind the boys. It was deafening.

"Not songbirds," Samson grimaced, dropping the blade of grass.

"Horrible scavengers and thieves." It occurred to Martin that Samson might think he was referring to Gypsies, so he rushed on, "My pa says they've ruined many a farmer, taking over corn and oat fields and diving at people like they'd peck your eyes out."

"Good eating though," Samson said. Martin tried to not look shocked. After an awkward silence Samson held his hand up, palm out to show it was empty. Then he reached behind Martin's ear and pulled out a coin. He handed over the buffalo nickel.

"How'd you do that?"

"My magic."

An older woman approached. Her beautiful gray hair was wound in loops at the back of her head in a way different from the Swedish braids Martin was accustomed to seeing. Her body looked old, lumpy, and stoop shouldered, but she still had a smooth face and young eyes.

She grinned at Samson and hugged him. They exchanged many words in their own tongue. Samson gestured at his clothes, which fit Martin generously, and to Martin's own clothes drying on the wire. Then Samson's grandmother turned and walked to Martin, picked up his hands in hers, and said in a heavily accented voice, "Thanks you to help my Samson from lake."

"It really wasn't necessary, ma'am." After all, Sam hadn't been drowning until he came along.

"Is the intention that matters—this I see." She squeezed Martin's hands. "Come. You eat."

Grandmother led them back into her wagon where she explained through Samson that she would set a small table inside for their lunch. Martin appreciated the chance to escape the probing eyes outside that watched his every movement. But inside was Ruby. Her set lip. Her constant staring at him. Her refusal to speak when he thanked her for setting a dish before them. She spoke only to the older woman, and although Martin didn't understand one word, the meaning was clear. Grandmother went about her tasks, replying calmly, "Is friend, is friend."

CHAPTER

Martin couldn't help but wish Pa could see this fine collection of horseflesh up close. He left in the late afternoon with dry clothes and a full belly. Samson's grandmother had done an odd thing when Martin said good-bye. She took his hands again and said, "I see you need help someday. We help you."

"She's just like that," Samson tried to explain as he walked with Martin back toward the lake. "Sometimes she tells people what she sees."

"She never turned my hands over to look at my palms," Martin said.

"She just knows; it's the second sight." Samson might long for a different life, but his trust in his grandmother's abilities was genuine.

Martin felt relief when Samson turned down an invitation to come to the farm and meet his family. The boy's eyes widened in fright. "I cannot go to your home."

"Not today, or they'd know I skipped school." Martin added half-heartedly, "But . . . maybe . . . another day."

"Not this day or any other." Samson shook his head. "I know where is school. I watch for you in the afternoons." He tugged a leather thong out from the neck of his shirt. "You I am giving this."

Martin held out his hand for the reverently offered necklace. It was tied around a small but perfect wooden horse.

"My grandfather cut it."

"He carved it." Martin offered it back. "I can't take this."
Likely Samson's grandfather was dead if he and his cousin
lived only with their grandmother. This might be his only
keepsake.

The boy's face clouded over just as it had earlier when
Martin had tried politely to claim he wasn't hungry. He
sensed he had to accept, that he would be violating a code of
manners if he didn't. "Thank you very much. I carve too. It's
very special."

Since he wasn't hungry Martin went straight to the barn. Not
that it was possible to discuss school problems with Ma or
Aunt Ida anyway. He missed his friends. He missed Stan's
mother who always talked to the boys as she fed them pie
or biscuits with jam and who had told Martin many times,
"You're family." He knew he could live with them in Stillwater,
if only he and Pa could get this farm paying in one season.

Why had Pa talked of this place so fondly? With the
weather warming, logging would end, and Pa would come
home soon. Their last conversation, long weeks ago, had
been right here in the barn before Pa hitched the horses and
went off to his winter work.

Pa had gestured with his empty pipe to an opening in the
ceiling. "Go up and have a look?"

They climbed to the hayloft on a makeshift ladder of
nailed planks. Morning light filtered through the roof boards.
They turned in slow circles in the large empty loft. A rare
moment alone with Pa. No doubt Pa studied the space with
a farmer's eye for the storage capacity, but Martin imagined
the summer of hard work that would be required to harvest
this much of anything.

They just stood together, looking up. Through the barn's
roof they saw the sky in several places. Martin was already

missing him, but Pa put little store in talking about feelings. He never said things like "I'm proud of you," but he would remark that Martin had gotten high marks that term or earned good money selling newspapers. Finally, in Gunnarsson tradition, they spoke of the work ahead.

"We've got some roof work to do this summer, son. I suppose my daddy built this barn. There was a sod stable before this. Have you seen it yet?"

Martin nodded. "There's not much left to see."

"There's not much of anything, true enough." Pa pointed with his pipe. "A few trunks and things in the corner yonder." There rested three small trunks and a wooden crate. Pa sat and fished in the crate of discarded items. He came up with a carved wooden gun, which he turned over in his hands, then took imaginary aim and fired. "I wonder if this was meant for me."

"What's in here?" Martin used his toe to lift the lid of a small trunk. He saw faded fabric and a blue book. He bent and opened the book, but the stiff pages fanned shut again. It was half filled with small handwriting.

"Some sort of farm ledger maybe. I'll give you the job of sifting through it all." Pa placed a hand on each knee and stood. "Maybe you'll find something Lilly can play with." Pa winked. "Or the family treasure. They say my mother came to this country with an inheritance, but I'm afraid we'll never know the truth of that story." Pa drew on his pipe as if it weren't empty, as if Ma hadn't forgotten to buy him tobacco when she stocked up on her own patent medicines. For a second it almost smelled right.

"Time to harness up and head for the logging camp."

Martin wished Pa didn't have to leave and wished he could say so. But he was no good at saying those things either. They'd never even talked about Dan's death. Not really. Pa would just say, "No sense fishing in water that's already gone downstream."

"Working at the logging camps isn't so bad." Pa believed

in putting a good face on things that couldn't be changed. "I'm lucky I have a way to earn a wage. But I hope our first crops can see us through the year, maybe even a little to sell for profit."

One year. "You think we can make this place pay?" Martin asked.

Pa laced his fingers together then stretched his arms as if he couldn't wait to do all the work. "We'll go at it hammer and tongs."

Martin loved the old blacksmith's expression that Pa used to say before tackling any large job. It felt good to hear it again, like the last year hadn't really happened.

"And after we do, we'll fight for something to keep us busy. I remember from when I was a boy how winters on a farm got powerful long. Long and silent. That's when the land speaks to you, in the silence."

When Pa pulled his wagon up to the porch, swung down, and hugged the women, Martin didn't know how to say good-bye. He yearned to jump up on the wagon seat and yell "boots and saddles" like he and Dan did as children when they went on adventures with Pa. It was easier to walk to the team and nuzzle Finn and Marshall and whisper good-bye to them than talk to Pa.

Noises in the farmyard caused the remembered scene with Pa to vanish. Martin arrived at the barn door just as Aunt Ida and Lilly came onto the porch. Ma was behind them, still in her housecoat. Before Dan died she never slept late, ever, but now she didn't fully dress some days at all.

"Lord, who in tarnation?" Aunt Ida said, hastily patting her white hair.

A large man on a wagon pulled up his horses, nodded to the ladies, and said, "I'm Robert Perry." He climbed down. Mr. Perry had a pudgy face and red hands, and an apologetic way about him. In fact his first words were to say he was sorry to take so many weeks to visit. He nodded at the porch, then turned to the barn. "This must be Martin. I'm one of the bachelors that raised your pa."

Martin knew there were two Mr. Perrys who had raised Pa. This one, who looked to be twenty years older than Pa, and Robert's father, who died last year. The family had never met them, but Pa always talked of the good life he had with them.

Mr. Perry shook his hand. "Your pa came by to see me on his way to the camps. I've been laid up since with the late winter ague."

Ma clutched her bedroom wrapper around her. After meeting Aunt Ida, Mr. Perry turned to Ma and spoke haltingly. "Ma'am, so nice to meet you finally. I sure haven't been one to put a pen to paper all these years. So, I'm late to say how sorry I am for your loss last year."

Ma just stared at Mr. Perry. Martin assumed she thought about Dan all day, every day. But now that someone actually referred to him, she looked blank. There was a time when Ma would have smiled at Mr. Perry's shyness. Later, *that* Ma would have said something to the family like "Isn't he the blushing bashful bachelor farmer." *This* Ma just nodded, then turned to go inside. Martin glimpsed her drag the spoon and cough syrup out of her pocket.

Months ago Pa had attended the funeral for Mr. Perry's father. That's when they made the plans for passing the Gunnarsson homestead back to Pa. Mr. Perry wanted to stop farming but would still live on his own place. He would give Martin's family a cow and the use of equipment and machinery to get their first crops started.

Tied to Mr. Perry's wagon was a milk cow he called Ella. Lilly stepped from behind Aunt Ida's skirts and danced across the yard to the cow's shoulder. She petted her gently, "Ella . . . Ella . . . Ella."

"My Lord," breathed Mr. Perry in a surprised way, as though he wasn't used to the sound of his own voice saying something he hadn't practiced. "Why, she's the spitting image."

Whose spitting image? Before Martin could ask who Lilly looked like, Mr. Perry had walked around the wagon and busied himself unloading a crate of laying hens. He set the box of murmuring chickens on the porch step with a nod to Aunt Ida. "Ma'am, if you can use them—with my father gone now, I want to get out of the chicken business entirely."

"Thank you." Aunt Ida nodded toward Lilly. "They'll provide plenty of work for the young lady."

"If there's anything I can do for the family . . ." Mr. Perry said, but trailed off as though he'd spoken his ration for the day.

Even Aunt Ida couldn't persuade him to stay for a cup of coffee. Mr. Perry gave a final awkward nod, cap in hand, before leaving.

Pa always spoke with such admiration of the Perrys' kindness that it was like meeting a distant grandfather. But this shy man couldn't be the fun-loving man Pa had told stories about. And who had Lilly reminded him of? It was as if Mr. Perry almost couldn't get away fast enough after seeing her.

CHAPTER

Each day passed slowly, but fresher scents of spring started to sweep away winter's memory. Sounds returned too. Flocks of birds hurried north in capital-V formations. About once a week, despite Pa's prediction that they'd never "catch on," the rickety-tick of an automobile carried up to the farmyard from the road. Except for mealtimes, sleeping, or school, Martin stayed outside or in the barn. He sometimes read to Ella, preferring the cow's company to the house full of women.

Glass had been expensive when the barn was built, so the main floor was always as dark as evening. Martin pulled the milking stool under the only window, where Grandfather Gunnarsson's old tool bench stood. They had found no books in the house when they moved in, though Ma had several past issues of the *Ladies' Home Journal*. In Stillwater he'd frequently borrowed library books, but here the nearest library was miles away.

Ever since Martin could remember he had learned reading and writing out of the McGuffey Readers series. He was now in the final reader of the familiar tan and red books. Their last assignment, "After the Thunderstorm," by James Thomson, wasn't so bad for a poem. Today Miss Abrams had hastily assigned the older students to "read on" in the

Sixth Eclectic Reader. Martin located Reading Selection VI, "House Cleaning," and read out loud:

> The walls are stripped of their furniture—paintings, prints, and looking-glasses lie huddled in heaps about the floor; the curtains are torn from their testers, the beds crammed into windows, chairs and tables, bedsteads and cradles, crowd the yard, and the garden fence bends beneath the weight of carpets, blankets, cloth cloaks . . .

He skipped ahead a page.

> These smearings and scratchings, these washings and dashings, being duly performed, the next ceremonial is to cleanse and replace the distracted furniture.

Ella lowed and turned a questioning eye. He scanned the dense descriptions of servants, scullery maids, and wheelbarrows filled with lime. God help him. "I'll stop." Martin patted the cow but didn't milk her yet. If he came in with the milk before supper was ready, Lilly would try to engage him in a game of checkers, or Aunt Ida would ask him to hold a hank of yarn on his outstretched hands while she rolled it into a ball, or he would try and fail to talk to Ma. The more patent medicines Ma took, the more she slept and the less she spoke to anyone.

Wasn't there a book of some sort in the old trunks he'd discovered with Pa? He climbed into the loft. The day's remaining light seeped in better up here. Cool evening air also crept in through many cracks in the walls, but it was almost warm enough to sleep out here.

Martin planned. He'd bring bedding and a lantern from the house. The loft wouldn't be fancy, but it would be a room of his own. Until it was brimming with hay in the fall, it would beat sleeping at Lilly's feet behind the kitchen stove. In the corner were the trunks Pa had told him to sort through. Martin pulled them into position to serve as a makeshift chair and bedside table. He opened the trunks before stacking them. One held clothing and an old quilt top—at least that's what they appeared to have been. Martin took out each item, piece by piece, until he saw the small hole in the trunk's corner where mice had gotten in and chewed the contents.

He was glad to be alone so he could study a yellowed muslin corset at the bottom of the trunk, smashed flat by the weight of clothing and years. Martin picked it up and separated the front from the back, rounding it out and giving it shape again. The string tie fell to the floor in pieces. He knew little of women's undergarments, having only seen them drying on wash day. Did it tie in the front, the back, or on the side? But he'd felt them. Plenty of times he'd helped Ma or Aunt Ida down from the wagon, his hands on her waist, and could feel the hard stays the corset held in place. It was like putting his hands around a tree trunk with ridges.

A length of twine held together six black buttons. More buttons, carved from shells, were sewn to an old dress bodice. He replaced everything, hoping Ma might be well enough to take an interest in the buttons someday.

Finding the undergarment among the tattered clothing made him willing to investigate further. He flipped the top on the third chest with a magician's flair, saying *Voila!* The gesture reminded him of Samson.

The third trunk held girl items. But no mice had gnawed their way in here. There was one very old doll with human hair, clothes, and quilts. These things might have belonged to his Aunt Cora. Best of all were a book and the crinkled handwritten ledger he had seen with Pa.

Martin grabbed the books and slammed the lid. The first was a volume of poetry. Some poems are interesting, Martin thought, thumbing through Longfellow, Wordsworth, Milton, and Shelley. But the rhyming lines of these reminded him of words from "House Cleaning," and he wanted to erase poem-like words like "smearings and scratchings" and "washings and dashings" from his memory.

Martin set the book down carefully. Obviously someone

had cared for it well. He figured he would do the same. The second was the wider but thinner book with its stiffened cover of blue fabric. Only half of the pages in the volume, hand bound with yellowing thread, were filled.

Pa had called it a farm ledger, but it looked more like a diary. Martin brought the volume closer to his face to study the script. Inside the front cover, in large flowing letters, was inscribed:

Presented to Cora Gunnarsson
on the Occasion of
Twelve Years of Life
19 March 1864

His aunt's diary! After that fancy first page Cora's letters were as small as fractions. She had written with no regard to the faint blue lines. It appeared she tried to use every quarter inch of space. Martin knew writing paper had been precious back then, and it was still scarce now. But he wondered how a girl, living on this farm, could have found so much to say. He read the first page.

My name is Cora Louise Gunnarsson. I live on this claim with my father and mother. A secret is that I think there will be a baby. I attend the neighborhood school where I have two friends, Jo and March. Next year there will be a raising bee for a school building. My parents speak in Swedish at home, but at school we never do.

Martin looked out the window into the darkening barn-yard. The baby she wrote about was certainly Pa. He felt a little dishonest, like he was spying on his father's childhood. The urge to read on pulled at him like an untamed horse pulls on a rope.

5 May 1864

*Daylight lasts so long now. We almost never light the rag that
Mother soaks in fat and sets in a can to burn for light. The boys
are gone from our little school for plowing and planting. Father
and Mr. Connor and the bachelor Perry work together again this
year. They are still plowing. Then they will harrow, cross harrow,
seed, and after harrow the fields. I think they might grow tired of
working the same squares of earth over and over, but I never tire
of walking their late afternoon lunch out to them. I am still at
school, so they must come to the house for the large noon meal.
We will soon have fun when the crops are planted.*

*Many homesteads need a permanent house. Several will go up
this summer and there will be many socials. Today Robert Perry
offered me cookies from the lunch I carried to the men. He should
know that women never eat the food they carry to the field.
Father said I blushed, and I think it is true.*

—Cora Gunnarsson, Minnesotan

Martin's head shot up in understanding. He knew a Robert
Perry. But the Robert Perry he knew was an old man—at least
twenty years older than Pa, which would have made him only
ten years or so older than Cora. He'd have been a young man
in his twenties at the time of this writing.

Ever since the early years at school Martin had a terrible habit. "You don't hurt anyone but yourself," his teacher
would say about his tendency to read the end of stories first.
Daylight failing by the minute, he flipped ahead to where the
script ended. While the earlier entries had been carefully
drawn on the page by a journalist who took time to be exact,
the entry for 6 July 1865 bounced on its page as if written in
a race.

6 July 1865

*Mother is sick. Not even Father was this sick. She told me to take
Jacob to the Perrys. Her last words were about a dowry, which I
hid safely in my doll's house. Jacob is starting to cry. I am afraid
to disobey her, but I am also afraid to leave her alone.*

Ice sluiced down Martin's spine just like when he'd jumped
into the cold lake and discovered Samson. His mind snapped
back to the book in his hand. Was this forty-year-old proof
that the family legend was true? If so, where was this fabled
treasure, this dowry that Cora hid? He had already explored
what remained of the homestead's few buildings.

Lilly's voice cut the silence and made Martin jolt and
bang his knee on the trunk lid. "Mother sent me to see if the
cow kicked you." As always she clutched her rag doll, Stella,
against her ribs. He had not seen her yet today; he'd left for
school before she was up and had been in the barn since
returning. She stared at him as if she expected something.

Martin's heart pounded from being surprised. "What are
you doing up here?"

"It's my barn, too." Lilly crawled fully into the loft, then
stood looking around. She pointed with her free hand. "What
are you reading?"

"I'd tell you if it were any of your business." He herded
her back toward the ladder. "Go on, unless you want to milk
the cow. Your arm will freeze that way if you don't ever put
down that stupid doll."

"Will not," she called over her shoulder. A few minutes
later he heard her through the barn wall, crying "I miss Dan,
I miss Dan."

Martin remembered how close Lilly and his older brother
had been, always teasing and laughing, while Martin usually
did both boys' chores. He carefully lit a lantern, hung it high
away from the bedding straw, and milked Ella.

22 June 1864

Mother said she brought something special from Sweden that her father made. Her older brother got their farm, but she got something else. She kept it with her every day of the long journey. I wonder what it can be. I certainly have seen every item we possess in this small house. My Swedish grandpa made Mother's wedding ring, but it is very plain. Perhaps she means something else.

CHAPTER

Thunk. Martin stooped, picked up another length of firewood, placed it on the chopping stump, and swung the heavy splitting ax. *Thunk.* He took care not to strike all the way through the chunk of wood, which would hasten the destruction of the handy stump—the firmly rooted base of an ancient tree.

Stoop . . . lift . . . swing . . . *thunk.* Martin loved chopping wood. It had been his job at Pa's livery stable, back before they lost it. But he still hated the small country school. Stoop . . . lift . . . swing . . . *thunk.* With every blow he imagined striking those damn Barker boys. They ridiculed him constantly for living on the worst farm in the county. They never let up about there being no horses on the place. Stoop . . . lift . . . swing . . . *thunk.* Martin was focused so intensely on punishing the wood that he didn't hear a man approaching.

"You're pretty good with that ax. For a boy."

Martin's swing went wild, landing hard in the stump. Trying not to appear startled, he turned slowly and saw a town man dressed in a white suit.

"How'd you come by here?" he asked, noting the absence of horse or wagon.

The man smiled. "I left my automobile out at the road." He looked close to Ma's age. "Is your father here?"

"No."

"Then who's in charge?"

"Of what?"

"I'm Mr. Meehan from the bank. I've brought some papers and things. Whom should I speak with?"

"My ma's in the house." Martin pointed past the man with his ax. He watched the city man pick his way through the farmyard, careful to protect his shiny shoes from chicken droppings. Martin was tempted to go to the road and see the automobile. He'd seen a few of the homemade contraptions in Stillwater, but they weren't common. Last year the newspaper reported there were only about eight thousand autos in the whole country. Pa said there would never be more automobiles than horses. There would always be work for a good farrier.

But remembering that Ma was taking cough syrup that morning, he decided to go to the house. Who exactly *was* in charge during Pa's absence? Certainly Ma couldn't handle much in the way of business now.

Lilly pranced around him at the door, clutching her rag doll. "We have company, Martin. Our first guest. Take off your muddy boots if you're coming in."

Martin squinted down at the small girl who lately gave more orders than his mother. Lilly wouldn't start school until next year. Besides leaving Stillwater and his friends, she was the other trial Martin suffered.

Martin squeezed into an oak ladder-back chair next to Lilly's place. He studied Mr. Meehan across the table, smelled his barbershop spice.

Aunt Ida poured coffee and set out the last of the sugar cookies. "All my life on a farm," she complained. "And when I finally get away, I'm brought back to the country in my old age." She had changed from her gray everyday apron to a fancy embroidered one.

Mr. Meehan was explaining to Ma that there was a loan on the farm. Mr. Meehan called it "a small but pressing mortgage. That's in addition to annual taxes, mind you. And fees."

Martin wondered why a banker had such a keen interest in this old place.

"Of course, if you forfeit—ah, that means if you don't pay the tax—then the bank gets the property."

Martin's head shot up. "We know what 'forfeit' means."

Mr. Meehan didn't ask Martin anything, or even acknowledge his presence. He just talked on and on. Ma occasionally nodded and said "Yes" or "I see."

"Just this week, three farmers in this area have forfeited." Meehan ate a cookie the size of a saucer in three bites.

"I see."

"I'm sure you'll want to tell your husband I stopped by. There *is* a Mr. Gunnarsson, isn't there?"

"Yes, I'll tell him."

"Then again, sometimes . . . I can find a buyer for a farm in trouble."

So he was a land buyer too. Martin pushed a cookie hard with his tongue against the roof of his mouth until the coarse sugar granules felt like sand; then, like always, he sucked milk through his clenched teeth to finish dissolving it.

Mr. Meehan ignored Martin, giving him plenty of time to study the man. "Last week some ruffians shot up Westergaard's barn. Likely Gypsies."

Aunt Ida clasped both hands to her flat chest. Martin hadn't told anyone about Samson and had seen the boy only once since meeting that day underwater. Martin had been on the road, being pestered by those blasted Barker brothers, and Samson, who was riding with several men, looked daggers at the Barkers but only slightly nodded to Martin.

Mr. Meehan went on, very slowly. He was a very polite speaker, even while delivering bad news. He frowned, saying, "Now the Westergaards want out." Then he smiled. "And they're in luck. I can sell that place for them." Meehan stopped smiling and molded his face to match the news he was bearing. Again he directed his comments to Ma: "If it should ever come to that here, that you want to sell the farm, I mean, well, I can help in many ways. Pardon my impertinence, Mrs. Gunnarsson, ah, Martha, ma'am, but ladies such as yourselves deserve the fineries a town has to offer . . . beautiful dresses and such."

"We'll be fine, Mr. Meehan." Ma spoke softly. "My husband won't be gone much longer."

Mr. Meehan rested his hand on Lilly's shoulder, then patted her doll Stella. "This little darling here would have proper friends close by, and your boy here—"

"Martin," Martin said.

Mr. Meehan went right on, "should have good schools."

Martin felt like he had two minds. On the one hand, he could dance with happiness that a man had come right out to this godforsaken farm offering to buy the place. On the other hand, he told himself, *Whoa, this farm is Pa's dream.* Besides, he didn't entirely trust the way Mr. Meehan said things. Martin watched the man study Ma's face. He hadn't looked at Ma's blue eyes and creamy skin in a long time. Ma hadn't inspired much notice lately. Martin was a bit surprised to see how beautiful she was. Under Mr. Meehan's gaze, a red flush slowly seeped into Ma's face from her yellow hairline.

Aunt Ida sprang up and quick as a bee sting handed Meehan several letters. "Mr. Meehan, would you please carry these to town to post?"

Martin flushed with fury. Last night, at the small kitchen table, he had written Chet and Stan a complaining letter about the farm, how boring school was, and how he planned to return after they harvested in the fall. Not only was the house so cramped that everyone knew everyone else's business, but now Aunt Ida had given the letter to Meehan. Martin could have posted it himself somehow in due time. He clenched his teeth so as not to object.

Mr. Meehan nodded. "I'll take care of it."

"I have to get back to my chopping." Martin decided to test whether he really needed manners out here. He stood abruptly. "I'll walk you out," he announced, adding, "you'll want to be getting back before dark." In his side vision Martin saw Lilly shake a finger at his rudeness.

12 July 1864

Mother was lonely until Mister Connor got a new wife. She came today and put mother's wedding ring on a length of thread. She suspended it over Mother's belly and after several minutes it started to sway. Mrs. Connor said this means the baby will be a boy. I listened from the loft. The women forgot they sent me there and not outside. The ring was hard to take off, and later did not go back on Mother's finger. She asked me to think of a safe keeping place. We wrapped it in a quilt square and pushed it between two logs.

I studied it in the sunlight first. It is signed with her father's metalsmith signature, a small design stamped inside. Mother explained the symbols. There is a crown with a sword that looks like a lightning bolt. It is all tinier than anything I've ever seen.

—Cora Gunnarsson, American Citizen

In the margin Cora had sketched the tiny design. Martin wondered what had become of the ring. He knew from school in Stillwater that Paul Revere had been a silversmith before his famous ride and that silversmiths signed their work with distinct miniature symbols. His text had even shown a sketch of the symbol Revere used.

He indulged in a daydream that his great-grandfather had made a silver horseshoe to send with his daughter to America. Or a gold cup. He smiled at these fairy-tale images but laid down the diary to have a good look around the place.

Since foreign money would do immigrants no good here, he asked himself what besides jewelry they might have brought over that was made of metal. If you were going to an unsettled land with few blacksmiths, you would need to bring your own necessary tools, like ax heads and saw blades, and you could fashion wooden handles for them once you got here. And if you planned ahead and wanted doors to swing properly, you'd likely pack hinges too, or you would be forced to nail leather straps onto doors as makeshift saggy hinges. Even nails and bolts had been scarce. Many cabins and barns were built without them, laboriously pegged and notched together.

Martin made the rounds of all the buildings. Nothing. The

small shed, corncrib, and chicken coop were literally slump-
ing into the earth from disuse.

Aunt Ida had taken Ma and Lilly out back to get up a garden plan. It was a rare thing for him to be alone in the house.
Finding the diary with its support for a hidden cache helped
him feel less ridiculous as he peered into his parents' bedroom, then Aunt Ida's tiny sleeping quarters behind a quilt.
He reminded himself that the diary also referred to a doll's
house, which hadn't survived the last four decades. Still, for
the sake of completeness, he explored the tiny loft over the
kitchen meant for drying and storing. Even the stove in the
house was just a stove. He searched it for a hallmark signature and found nothing but rust and soot. Ma's flatware and
pans were just tin and iron.

He headed to the barn, passing the chopping block. Out
of habit, he braced his feet against the armlike roots that
radiated from the massive stump. But this time he picked up
the ax only to examine its head. Ordinary.

As usual, no matter the time of day, the barn was dark.
Mice had long ago removed every useful sprig of straw and
hay from the main floor. He cataloged what was still there,
everything that contained even a bit of metal. A scattergun
barrel—on close inspection he saw that it was stamped with a
U.S. patent number. A pitchfork. He inspected the fork's tines
in the waning window light. Nothing. No stamp, no signature, nothing bearing the symbol that Cora had drawn.

He saw it when he left the barn and came back into daylight. The barn door hinges. Old, dark, and triangular. A set
of three, heavy and well made. On the left plate of each hinge
he could barely discern the familiar crown and thunderbolt,
proof that these had been brought by his grandparents with
this specific use in mind. He touched the design on two
hinges—it matched the sketch in Cora's diary, but rust had
completely destroyed it on the third. Rust wouldn't happen
to gold or silver. He recognized the error in his thinking:
precious metals were too soft to serve as utilitarian items.

He couldn't resist rubbing the pad of his forefinger over the tiny engraving and picturing the great-grandfather who'd made this exact hinge—in a different time, a different century, a different country entirely.

Martin pushed back from the dinner table and said, "I'm not sleeping in the kitchen by Lilly anymore. She's always talking to herself and humming."

"Maybe it's you she's talking to." Aunt Ida let her words settle a bit. Lately Aunt Ida seemed to be testing Ma, giving her more work to do and drawing her into conversation. "What do you think, Martha?"

"That's fine."

But when Martin retrieved the last armful of his belongings, Ma asked, "Martin, where are you going with all that?"

"I'm sleeping in the barn. I told you."

"Why, dear? What about the chickens?"

"The hayloft, Ma. I'll be up where it's clean and dry. Just until we get the hay in and it turns cold again." Martin looked straight into Ma's eyes. His gaze was no longer level to hers. He had grown. There was a time when she would have been the one to observe this. She looked back with empty eyes. Did she see Dan in him? Would she ever be Ma again?

Lilly distracted him by saying something over and over. It hit him that Lilly had no friends here either. Ma's strangeness must be all the harder on a small girl. These months on the farm she'd taken to playing "fancy lady comes visiting" under the back window. From this favorite spot she announced a third time, "Someone's driving up," before getting anyone's attention.

A curious wagon strained up the hill toward the house.

"Is it a notion wagon?" Aunt Ida squinted into the setting sun. "Weather's fair enough for dry goods sellers."

But this wasn't the square wagon with outside drawers that most notion sellers used. There were no pots, pans, and chairs tied to the sides for sale. This vehicle's rounded top resembled an old covered wagon. A little porch roof extended forward over the seat. Except for the plain brown color, it looked like a Gypsy wagon.

The driver mopped his dusty forehead with a beefy arm. Martin nodded and was about to offer water for him and the horse when a crash rang from the house and a voice shouted, "It's them Gypsies. Count the chickens. Tie the cow." Aunt Ida, brandishing a rolling pin like a bayonet, marched out to the edge of the porch. The heels of her shoes smacked the wooden floorboards with each step.

"Come away from there, Martin." She sounded so angry, Martin looked again to see if she maybe had a gun. Even with no real weapon, Aunt Ida could strike terror in the hearts of ten men with just her voice.

The driver stood and showed his two empty hands. "I assure you ma'am, I am neither a Gypsy nor a ne'er-do-well." He gestured to the side of the wagon. "As you can see, I am a photographer. There is just enough afternoon light, and I wondered if the family would like to sit for a portrait?"

Aunt Ida descended the steps and marched with her head thrust forward, leading with her spectacles. "That's a Gypsy wagon," she pointed accusingly.

The man bowed low. "Very perceptive, madam, and a finer travel accommodation I have never known. Come and see."

Inside was a brightly decorated miniature home. A bed stretched across its width, behind the wagon seat. The chimney pipe of a small cookstove rose through the roof on the left wall. On the right side were doors and cupboards. Wooden crates of glass bottles, photographic equipment, and tripods were neatly arranged on the floor space in the center.

"I left the inside as it was when I bought it, though I've painted the outside to tame it down somewhat." The man smiled at Aunt Ida. "I'm Axel Stone."

"This here's the Gunnarsson place," Aunt Ida replied. "I'm the missus's aunt. Ain't never been this close to a Gypsy wagon before; they're right clever planned, I'll grant you that."

"Allow me to show you my work." He carefully pulled out a crate of portraits with thin boards packed between each for protection. Martin and Aunt Ida looked at them all. In portraits, families had included a favorite horse or dog or cat. If the homes had a porch, they sat on the stoop with taller members standing beside the steps. Always the house itself was pictured, and if it lacked a porch, the family arranged themselves on straight-backed chairs set in the yard for the occasion. In one photograph of a very large family, a portrait of a young boy was held between two siblings to mark the place he had held in the family before his early death.

Martin wondered what Axel Stone said to ensure that no one ever smiled. Behind the dogs in most pictures was a blurred area where their tails had wagged during the long exposure.

Ma joined the group and studied the portraits over Martin's shoulder. "They're lovely, Mr. Stone." Ma read aloud, "Stone's Throw Photography," which was painted like a sunrise on the wagon.

Mr. Stone tipped his hat. "Ma'am," he said formally, "how about a portrait of your family?"

Ma's face shut down at the mention of the family.

"We need to paint our house first," Aunt Ida said.

Mr. Stone tipped his hat. "Another time then." He settled into the seat and bent toward Aunt Ida. "Ma'am, I've heard tell the Gypsies are in and around this area." He winked, then added, "I don't know if there's anything to fear from them, but I assure you, they turn a wagon into a fine home."

At supper Aunt Ida muttered about barn burnings and horse thieves. She pointed to Lilly with her gnarled index finger and warned, "When Gypsies are in the area, you must be careful. They steal children. They'll take the laundry right off the line or a plow out of the field at the noonday break."

Lilly's eyes grew big as stove lids. In a tiny voice she asked, "How do you know if it's a Gypsy and not just a person?"

"They're shiftless people, got no homes, just travel in caravans like Mr. Stone's wagon. They're dark-skinned and dress fancy, and they speak their own language. Not natural talk, downright mysterious. Sometimes I think it's a pity shame God put so many different kinds in this world."

Martin wondered how many Gypsies his great-aunt had actually met. He had found meeting Samson's family to be interesting at least. He tried to steer her away from the topic. "Let's have a sitting when Pa gets back."

It was Aunt Ida's night to talk the ear off a mule. "My family didn't have daguerreotypes when I was a girl. Not even tintypes. Back then an artist went farm to farm and painted a picture of the place. He'd set his chair on a hill where he could see the entire yard." She gestured wide with her fork, "house, barn, everything. Took half a day. He'd paint it all."

All evening Martin looked forward to his first night in the barn. He even submitted to a rare game of checkers with Lilly, who was always willing, even though Martin won every time. He strolled out when just enough twilight remained to light the way through the barn's main floor to the loft where he'd left a lantern. He didn't bother to light it but lay down on a folded blanket, covered with two quilts, and sighed with joy at being alone.

He thought of Pa returning and all the work that lay ahead. The original chicken coop was gone, and they needed to build another. Of course, there were crops to plant. He imagined their great success as farmers would hasten his return home to Stillwater. Certainly one good year would earn them enough for him to buy a horse. He drifted to sleep picturing a tall chestnut with a black mane and tail.

Martin sneezed himself awake in the middle of the night. Blinking into complete darkness, he slowly recognized the noises and scurrying sounds within the barn's creaking walls.

He sat up, wide-awake. Even the rooster hadn't started his racket yet. With care he felt for the matches and lantern.

Out here he was his own man. He could read Cora's diary without feeling embarrassed. It wasn't that he enjoyed the girl's writing, he told himself, but that he had always been good at ciphers and puzzles. That's why he needed to study up on her life. She'd been so happy on this farm. Martin reached for the diary. He shoved a trunk over to his bedding and leaned against it. From this higher perch the lantern hissed and threw a thicker light.

We have just arrived home after a full day's journey from our visit to the Morrows. Everywhere their shelves are lined with objects. Mother says they have more things because they moved here from Ohio. People who come from the east have more than the immigrants. They have more clothes and lanterns and cooking implements. They even have more rags to use as cleaning cloths. They light a candle every evening.

Martin tried to school his mind into reading carefully for clues, but he kept getting lost in the story of Cora's life. Martin thumbed ahead, choosing paragraphs here and there, anticipating an entry announcing his father's birth. The last entry he had time to read discussed gathering wildflowers. He marked his place with a pressed flower, one of several that cascaded from the volume whenever he picked it up. The morning sun leaked in through cracks in the walls and ceiling, warming the barn's smells and illuminating the heavy air, which swirled with floating particles of dust and hay. He turned down the wick and dressed for another day.

I also sorted through Mrs. Morrow's button collection. Mother says hers in Sweden was as fine! She left many behind, since several sets would do nicely (them going from shirt to shirt or shirtwaist to shirtwaist as the clothing is replaced). My friend March gave me six jet buttons for a gift on my birthday last. I have not used them yet, preferring to hear them rattle in the tin where I save them.

—Miss C. L. Gunnarsson

CHAPTER

8

Martin looked forward to tilling season with Pa so he could quit school and work in the fields. In the country girls stayed in school later in the spring than boys, who were indispensable on the farm. But it was still the "season of mud and ruts," and none of the boys had quit yet.

Walking home from school, he met no one on the county road for half a mile. Then Frank Barker and his younger brother, Dale, came racing across a field on their horses.

The Barker boys weren't twins but looked alike. They teamed up well to intimidate, and even Miss Abrams gave them a good leaving alone. They bounced up to Martin on their mounts. "What'sa matter, Martin? Horse pull up lame today?" Frank taunted.

Dale pulled his horse in tight so that the two animals flanked Martin who walked steadily forward. He studied them on either side. The boys' coats were newer than his own, which was patched but pressed. Theirs were dirty and unkempt. Martin wondered if they had a mother. For the first time he appreciated Aunt Ida's help to Ma.

"Hey, town boy. Don't nobody live around here without horses. Ain't your pa a farrier to boot?"

Frank chuckled. "Yeah, that's kinda like the baker's son having no bread." The boys edged their horses closer, trying to crush Martin between them.

"What's your name again?" Frank jerked his horse side-
ways, even closer. "I remember now. Goonerson. If Anderson
means son of Anders, and Carlson is son of Carl, you must
be the son of a goon."

Martin saw that the saddles the boys used were in a sorry
state of disrepair. The animals' feet lurched dangerously
close to his own. The buckle above Frank's stirrup scratched
Martin's left arm. Martin longed to yank that foot out of the
stirrup and pull the boy to the dirt road.

"You sure have been a disappointment, Goony. Your
lunches ain't hardly worth stealing." Dale kicked the pail out
of Martin's hand. "Cold boiled potatoes."

Martin could ignore taunts, but no one took anything
away from him without a fight. Planning to fish on his way
home from school, he'd brought a short pole concealed under
the extra shirt he carried. Martin took it in both hands and
held it across his chest. He wouldn't need to strike the horses
or boys with it. The stick was only slightly longer than the
width of Martin's body, but the next time the boys brought
the horses slamming into him, the pole's ends rammed their
flanks. They reared their heads and separated. He'd seen Pa
use this trick when entering a stall where an unusually large
or unruly animal was tethered. Pa kept a stick only slightly
wider than himself, which he'd whittled to a dull point at one
end. Edging toward the horse's head, he'd scrape the stick
along the wallboards so that if the animal tried to crush him
against the stall, it would jab itself and sidle away.

The boys repeated the maneuver twice more without
realizing Martin's tactic. The second time, Frank's gelding
kicked off to the side of the road, snorting. He glared backward with an almost disgusted look at his rider.

Now at the Perry fields, Martin hopped onto a fence rail
and swung his legs over. The rebellious boys thought better than to attempt the jump and whipped their mounts off
down the road. The stupid Barkers hadn't figured out what
he'd done, and it gave him satisfaction to know he'd bettered
them.

Martin thought about Sam. He decided to hike over to the Gypsy meadow after checking in at home. He approached the house through the back fields and entered the garden door. Not having seen Mr. Meehan's automobile, he was surprised to find the man in the front room. Ma held the hem of her apron in one hand and rested her chin on the other. She sat, head bowed, in her sewing rocker, and it didn't take Martin long to piece out that she'd been crying.

"Ma?" he said.

She held out her arm to him. "Mr. Meehan brought out a telegram from town," she said. "Your pa had an accident and won't be able to come home for a long time."

The rocker was so low, Martin knelt by his mother to bring them face-to-face. The chair had no armrests so that a woman's arms would be free while doing needlework. She looked terribly sad now with her fingers limp in her lap. He took a mangled scrap of onionskin paper from her hand, unfolded it, and read:

```
Logging chain snapped. Broke Jacob's leg. Traction.
Unable to move 6 weeks or more. Dr. B. Castleman.
```

He straightened, placed a hand on her shoulder, and said, "That's lucky. Pa's *lucky,* Ma. He's always telling me about men getting killed when one of those chains lets fly."

Meehan put in vaguely, "If I can help in any way with the farm . . ."

"I should go to him," Ma said softly.

"Anything I can do to help, Martha."

Martin held up a flat hand to silence the man. "I'll be the one to go, Ma. Mr. Perry will want to help. He can bring me to town tomorrow, and I'll wait for a freight wagon out. I have to be the one to go; I'll need to bring back the horses."

Martin strode to the door and held it open for the banker.

"Thank you for bringing out the telegram, Mr. Meehan. We'll be just fine now."

Aunt Ida and Lilly came inside with armfuls of crab apple branches to bloom indoors. Worry was written on Aunt Ida's face. She had clearly been distracting Lilly, and not for the first time, Martin felt thankful for her presence here with them. He explained he was going to get Mr. Perry's help. Lilly, with tear-stained cheeks, mumbled repeatedly, "I want my daddy."

27 May 1864

There is a war. It is not in Minnesota. The news we get is always old, and passed from Mrs. Perry. She sends newspapers through her son, Robert. Pa talks of going to fight when the crops are in. They are fighting other states in the country. Pa says unification is an important cause. "Unification is as important to the country as freedom is to the individual." Minnesota became a state only six years ago. I have never seen Pa fight.
                                                                        —Cora Louise

CHAPTER

M r. Perry came with his team at first light. Aunt Ida and Ma saw Martin out to the wagon with pails of food, including many of Pa's favorites. There was also a jar of buttermilk and a loaf of braided bread with currants for Martin to share with Mr. Perry on the way to town.

The first mile they rode in silence, encountering nothing more than morning songbirds and one red fox. Martin stole glances at the man he knew as the object of Aunt Cora's long-ago girlhood affections. Mr. Perry, at sixty-two, was nicely rounded everywhere—a round nose, fat belly, and beefy fists. His size tipped the springs under the wagon seat in his direction, making Martin feel he would slide left on the seat if he didn't occasionally reposition himself against gravity.

Martin could picture Mr. Perry as a young man from Cora's diary descriptions. He wanted to ask Mr. Perry about his aunt and the people and things that she wrote about. But he was not about to admit to reading a girl's diary.

Over and over Mr. Perry sneezed. He reached into a wooden bucket by his feet, wrung out a cloth in cold water, and tied it over his nose and mouth, cowboy style.

"Ever since I was a boy," Mr. Perry said, "I've had a sensitivity to this time of year. Some say it's weeds or certain trees; I don't rightly know. But come a certain week each spring I can't hardly stand to be outdoors."

Pa once told Martin how Robert Perry suffered like this every year. Martin knew he could rely on the man like an uncle, but he wouldn't ask him for help on the farm.

As they drove along, Mr. Perry rinsed his breathing cloth in the spring water whenever the sneezing started again. After an hour he handed Martin the reins and swung the cloth in the air to cool it off, then rode a ways with it pressed onto his red eyes.

Almost nothing but a feather tick made Martin sneeze. He thought to distract Mr. Perry with conversation and asked, "Mr. Perry, do you remember when my pa was a boy?"

"Why, I surely do." Smile lines shot out from the doughy folds surrounding his eyes. "I must've been twenty or so, and it was a novelty for me to have so small a boy around. My sainted mother doted on Jacob until she died when Jacob was ten."

Martin hissed softly to the horses.

"I reckon we did all right by Jacob at that. I remember when Jacob was a little tad, he decided it was money he needed more than anything. That boy begged and begged for a job until my pa spilled the cooking pepper out onto the oilcloth and told him to pick the fly specks out of it." Mr. Perry grinned and shook his head in memory. "Damn if Jacob didn't spend all afternoon sifting through that pepper looking for fly specks. The boy fooled us though; we ended up paying him a whole dime piece."

Martin laughed at the story. He missed time alone with a man, occasionally saying cuss words and not worrying about what the women thought. He decided to ask, "What about my grandpa, what became of him?"

"Your pa never told you much about him?"

"No, sir. He talked plenty of you though."

"Well, your grandpa Carl died of war wounds or some such sickness. He got home first though. Seems many died that way after the war. Then before your grandma Anna could decide what to do with the homestead, she and Cora died of the diphtheria. We took over the Gunnarsson place and farmed it some. Then last year, my pa took to bed, and Lord knows I couldn't do another planting, so I offered it back to your pa."

They drove in silence until Martin mustered the courage to ask, "What was *she* like? My Aunt Cora, I mean?"

Mr. Perry sat hard against the backrest. He had not sneezed in a time; still, he wiped his face and eyes thoroughly, then bent forward to dip the cloth up and down in the water. "Well, now, she . . . she was a fine girl." He looked up into the treetops as they passed through a stand of hardwoods. "She sewed fine things, all the time. She'd make doll clothes and give them away to little girls around here. I think she had made just about everything for the new baby. For Jacob. After . . . well, my mother would study those clothes when she dressed the baby and sometimes weep over the fine handiwork." He shook his head and stared into the water. "I remember Cora walked lunches out to the field for us. Her ma was too big with child that last season. Cora sat at the start of a row and she'd be sewing something, and every time we turned she'd wave. She'd sit like that and watch a time; then we'd turn and she'd be gone."

Martin didn't say anything. He didn't want to stop the memories.

"She was the image of your own sister, and that's a fact."

Again he considered telling the man about Cora's diary, but thought better of it. "Some say my grandma had a fortune and that she died before telling anyone where it was."

"Oh, a dowry, a Swedish dowry. Yes, my mother believed that story. Maybe Anna told her, I don't know." He nodded his head in a way that could have meant the story was true, or that he had heard it but it was just a story, or that the entire thing was foolishness. It wasn't clear what he thought, so Martin waited for him to find more to say.

"It was a common enough practice to give money to girls headed to the new country. Often their young husbands didn't even know the amount until they arrived. Then they would exchange their Swedish *riksdaler* for American notes, and that's when the husband would see how many hundreds his wife had. Maybe even a thousand or more. I never heard that Anna surprised Carl by exchanging any money when they landed. Either she didn't have cash, or she kept the Swedish currency."

Mr. Perry slapped his knee. "It's likely just a tale that follows from the old country. Folks bring their stories of trolls and leprechauns and such. My pa and I and Jacob never set store in it, no more 'n' Jacob believes those Paul Bunyan stories the lumbermen tell. Folks just need a good yarn now and then is all."

Ahead, wagons coming from town had been turning into a driveway, and as they approached Martin read a sign:

BANK
SALE
AUCTION

He looked at Mr. Perry. "If you don't mind, I'd like to go."

They turned the team, walked up to the farmyard, and joined a crowd that was forming around the hand pump. Everything that belonged inside the house was outside. Two men stood like preachers in a wagon bed with their congregation of mostly men—farmers and townspeople—fanned about in the yard. Those from town clustered together in shade cast by the barn. Mr. Meehan relaxed among them, watching the proceedings.

They were almost finished with household items. The auctioneer would point to an item, holler its name and a few details, and the bidding would begin. The other man helped him spot the folks who raised a hand to signal an offer. Things sold quickly.

A davenport.

A wardrobe.

Large items sold individually; others were grouped. Stacked in a wash boiler were an ironing board, butter churn, and dasher.

A bushel basket of dishware.

The family stood to one side, watching. Martin wondered what the bank would and would not take. Could the mother keep the eyeglasses she was wearing? The dog? Would they have to walk out of here?

The sale had been neatly and logically organized and now proceeded to tools and implements. Martin followed Mr. Perry, who circled behind the crowd.

"That there's a disc harrow," Mr. Perry said. "It's used to break up the earth after plowing. And that's a sulky plow. A very modern piece of equipment. Lets you ride like you're going to church instead of having to walk behind and steer the plow yourself. I might still be farming if I had that."

"Maybe you could get it cheap today."

"Even at ten cents on the dollar, I won't profit off a neighbor."

"You know these people?"

"Doesn't matter."

They left. But the family's image wouldn't leave Martin's mind. Two boys (the youngest clutched a blanket scrap as tightly as Lilly clutched her doll), mother, and father. And that father had two good legs.

25 June 1864

Mother never speaks to me of the baby that is coming. I know she is with child because I remember when we lived in with Mrs. Berg to wait for Ole to be born. Mrs. Berg looked this same way. Then one morning, they showed me something small and said the baby came in the night. Even on their borning day, babies have ten finger and toenails. I unwrapped Ole and checked right off.
—the future Mrs. Cora ????

CHAPTER

"Why did you want to go?" Mr. Perry asked.

"Mr. Meehan." Martin shook his head in disgust. "He's come around, talking about selling. Talking about foreclosures. I've been wondering what it means, is all."

"Meehan's no farmer," Mr. Perry said. "He made me an offer for my farm and yours too. I couldn't rightly let the place go to the likes of him without offering it back to Jacob first. That's right about a loan. It's small but we bought the property outright when Carl and Anna died. They didn't own it since they didn't live on it the five years required to prove up the claim. They call those relinquishments, and they happened all the time with homesteads for lots of reasons."

Martin said, "He just buys up all the land and everything next to it! But he's a man who wouldn't even know which end of a chicken the feed goes in."

Mr. Perry thought a while. "God makes all kinds, but the world has a hand in it, too. Roger Meehan was orphaned like your pa when he was a boy. He's a fancy dandy now, but he had a time, too. Most people do—they have a refining time; they have difficulties."

"What happened to him?"

"Meehan worked out. Not uncommon for a boy, but he was powerful young. He started sweeping for the banker, who taught him the value of a dollar. I wonder, should we have done more for him like we did for Jacob? It's just so easy to see the need with a baby. Meehan may have finished his growing in town, but maybe he didn't grow up with much society. The society of a family is a powerful thing."

Martin knew what the last year had felt like with his own mother so withdrawn from him.

Mr. Perry said, "Now he's just a man with a plan, like many. Meehan already bought up Connor's old place."

Martin knew that name from Cora's diary. The Connors . . . homesteaders too . . . *Mother was lonely until Mister Connor got a new wife.* Maybe it was time for their old place to go, too. There was much to think about. He longed to take Samson's horse out of his pocket. It had already become something of a habit to rub it between his fingers. But he didn't want to explain about his encounter with the Gypsies to Mr. Perry. He would tell Pa all about that day; Pa didn't share Aunt Ida's crazy fear. And Pa would love seeing the perfectly proportioned miniature horse. It was sculpted from some unknown wood, the last possible color that brown could be before it's actually black. It fit in his palm, but there was no mistaking the powerful neck and chest. Deft turns from someone's knife suggested a snip of color between the nostrils and subtly articulated shoulder and hip lines from the flank. If only he could carve like that. He had tried carving horses, but they always had legs as straight as chair legs.

In town the general store manager agreed to help Martin find a ride in the direction of the logging camp. Martin accepted the man's offer to unload a freight wagon in trade for dinner and two bits worth of hard candy, Lilly's favorite. It was the first time he had thought to bring her anything. It felt like something Dan would have done. Martin remembered Dan's easy way with Lilly, always picking her up and swinging her around. He wondered if Mr. Perry had brought candy to Cora Gunnarsson, who died so long ago before she even had a chance to live.

Martin spent two days and nights with a teamster who delivered him eleven miles from Pa's logging camp. He set out on foot and arrived at the camp before five o'clock. The logging foreman who greeted him looked happy that he had come.

"Your pa is the best farrier this company ever saw." The little man swung his powerful arms as he walked briskly through the camp. "Damn drunk Irishman driving those teams of oxen didn't know what he was doing. Now, boy, the doctor says this can go either way. It might be your pa heals all right. And it might be he stoves up good." He shook his head. "Still can't hardly picture Jacob lame."

The short man managed to walk so fast that Martin, exhausted, had trouble keeping up. But he wasn't too tired to mistake the stench of the camp's winter garbage piles that were ripening everywhere in the warm sun.

"Visit with you will do him a world of good. He's in here."

Pa lay in a small square building made from the abundant pines of the area. The log walls were roughly hewn, and the slab floor was swept but had never been scrubbed. Martin had walked all day without stumbling, but the sight of Pa's yellow, waxy skin made him miss a step. He approached the cot slowly, not knowing what to say.

"He's on laudanum, boy. It helps him rest proper."

"Thank you. I'll just sit with him a while." The little man left, and Martin unpacked the sack of bed linens Ma sent. Presently he became aware of his father's eyes on him.

"Martin."

"Hi, Pa." Martin stood formally, his cap in his hand. Pa looked awful—but not dead. Anything was better than dead. As they spoke Pa sounded like himself. At least at first.

"You've grown," he whispered.

"It's just been a few weeks."

"Isn't this something?" Jacob gestured toward his legs with his large hands.

"Wasn't your fault, Pa. You're always warning me about the horses, and how this can happen when a chain snaps. We were lucky."

Pa shook his head in disbelief. "Lucky."

"Pa, you're gonna mend fine. You always told me, 'What doesn't kill, hardens.'"

"I don't know as that applies to bones."

Martin caught sight of a large dressing with pink drainage. "Leg break open, Pa?"

"Bones stuck straight out," Jacob said. "Doctor had quite a time with them. Won't let me go home for a good while."

"That's what the telegram said. That's why I came, to see you and to bring the horses home."

For a flash, Pa looked alarmed. But like milk vanishing in coffee, his concern was quickly swallowed by pain.

"You know I can handle them. You can't hire them out here anyway with the ice gone. Better we have them at the farm than pay for their keep here."

Pa squeezed his eyes shut. "The farm."

"Don't worry." The words sounded false as soon as Martin whispered them.

"I was so happy to be home on my folks' place." Pa's hands went limp on his stomach.

Martin snatched back his own hand from reaching out to cover Pa's. He was about to say they could sell the farm or explain about Mr. Meehan finding a buyer. But Pa didn't hear Martin try to interrupt him. He didn't hear Martin when he said, "We can always go back home."

"I might not be able to work."

The injury did look like it could change Pa's life. Martin hadn't thought about that. Farming was one thing, but what if Pa couldn't work out next winter as a farrier?

"I knew the farm was never right for Dan. But you, I thought you would love the land." Pa rested a minute.

Love the land? Pa didn't know how much Martin missed Stillwater.

"Farming is hard work, digging and inching across the dirt." Pa's whisper became even quieter. "But then one day you plunge your hands into a sack of seeds . . . the best moment. Like holding tiny specks of the future. I thought you would see farming with my eyes."

They had never spoken like this. Martin stood silent, wondering what else Pa would reveal. He scoffed at what he had been thinking on the trip here: that Pa would be sitting up in bed with a bandage on his leg, that Martin would tell him about home and the crazy meeting with the Gypsies. The laudanum made Pa say those things about loving farming, but the parts about Dan . . . he didn't like being compared to his brother. His older, perfect, fun-loving brother.

But no more came. Martin stayed in the little shed, checking throughout the night that Pa was still breathing.

In the morning Martin ate breakfast with the men in the mess tent. He visited a time with the horses, Finn and Marshall, then returned to Pa's bunk and found the doctor there. Dr. Castleman wanted Pa to remain sedated. He promised to remind Pa in the days ahead that Martin had visited.

The doctor's last words stayed with Martin during the two days it took to get back to the farm. "You're just burning daylight here; your pa won't remember anything you talk about anyway." But Martin was quite certain *he* would never forget.

4 July 1864
Mother prepares more for Father's leaving than for the coming baby. She knits socks and sews new shirts even though he promises to be home before winter.
—C. Louise Gunnarsson

CHAPTER
11

Having skidded logs all winter, Finn and Marshall were restless at first with the lazy pace of just pulling an empty wagon. Martin needed a heavy hand to restrain the horses as they started the trip back to the farm—his prison all winter. He tried not to think about the truth that now, instead of one, he had two parents who needed him desperately.

What had Pa said? *I knew the farm was never right for Dan. But you, I thought you would love the land.* Pa was right about Dan, but why would he think of Martin as a man of the land? Martin thought back and tried to remember things about Dan so he wouldn't forget. His brother was ambidextrous; he wrote the left half of a line with his left hand, then switched the pencil to his right to finish. He had the nicest singing voice in the family. Dan was always focused on the world around him, always going, always testing and teasing.

In the last of the light Martin retied the grazing horses near spots of fresh grass. He stretched out under the wagon when darkness fully came. He played in his mind how fun it would be if Stan or Chet were along, or even Samson. Then he told himself the truth. His mind had turned to Samson first. It was hard to believe they had met only weeks ago, so much had happened. He'd try to find Samson tomorrow after school—but no. That was the one good thing about Pa's accident: he wouldn't be going back to school now. He'd have to find some work to do. His family's survival depended on him.

By the time Martin arrived home the following night, he ached to climb the ladder to his loft bed but figured his mother might have waited up for him.

Ma sat at the table in a dim pool of light, her limp hands doing nothing. Absolutely nothing. She used to rock the churn with her foot, stitching in hand, while she recited sums with Lilly.

"Ma?"

She didn't say a word but stood and folded her hands in front of her apron, a question in her eyes.

"Pa's gonna be fine. I saw him twice. Talked with him." Martin didn't bother to mention that Pa objected to his taking the horses and that he had left with the animals while Pa was heavily dosed. "He sent the horses back with me."

"And down the line?" Ma whispered.

"I'll bring you back when I go get him." Martin hadn't asked the doctor when, so he invented: "In just a month or so."

"Perhaps . . . he could recover better, in the long term, I mean . . . if we were back in town."

How Martin used to long to hear those very words.

Ma looked as if she expected Martin to be pleased. "Stillwater. We could go back to Stillwater."

"What made you think of this?" he asked wearily.

"It's not like we don't have options. Mr. Meehan could arrange it at the bank."

Martin's heart started pounding. "You spoke to him about Pa?"

"We need to pay over eight hundred dollars by this fall."

"Maybe we don't have to pay it all off this year," Martin said.

"Mr. Meehan says it's best. Where will that kind of money come from?"

Martin had no idea. He found himself saying, "I could get a job."

"Where can you earn that much? Mr. Meehan can arrange it so we keep a little money if we let go now."

"Meehan! Money!" Martin had to struggle not to raise his voice to his mother. And he had to struggle not to accept the offer that she dangled. Before noon tomorrow he could have the family neatly packed back into the wagon and on their way home. It was so tempting. Just what he had wanted. But what he said was, "More than money, Pa needs this place. Everyone died on him here forty years back. He needs to see life around this place."

Martha walked around her son and pulled a tin plate of food for him from the back of the stove, then filled a hand basin with hot water from the reservoir.

"Or," Martin paused, slicing into a potato, "the money could come from farming. This *is* a farm. I guess this is what we do now." Like it or not.

"What do you know about farming?"

"Mr. Perry can tell me what I need to do. Every step."

"But what if there's no rain this year. Or too much rain. Or locusts or . . . anything." Martin knew that Ma's agricultural knowledge was limited to Bible references.

He remembered the farm sale. "Ma, this place is worth more than we would get from Meehan. These buildings Grandpa built aren't much, but the fields are good. Mr. Perry said that the timber that's not logged off—we've got good conifers and hardwood—is worth more than we owe. We could go back to Stillwater and I could work, but we don't have a house to go back to, and Meehan's money wouldn't buy us one."

With effort Martin lowered his voice. He didn't want to wake up Lilly or Aunt Ida. He and his mother agreed that for the time being they would stay put for Pa. For one year. It was no different from what Martin had secretly promised himself: to give the farm exactly one year. Only now he would be working it alone.

After eating he went to the hayloft. As restless as the horses on a cold morning, he picked up Cora's diary to read before turning down the lantern.

17 July 1864

I was left alone with my friend March while Mother and Father went to the Koch funeral. We children must not attend for it was a case of diphtheria. And they will keep well back from the man whose family, his wife and three children, awoke two days ago, became ill, and died before sunset. I entertained March by playing store. We set up barrels in the barn, upside down, so that a small pile of stones atop one resembled a keg brimming with crackers. To imitate a barrel of flour, we used sand. March was very happy with the game, pretending to sell the cat and kittens as livestock.

21 July 1864

*I play school in my doll's house to escape the afternoon heat.
I dream that one day we will have a wooden school building
instead of Stornsteen's old dugout with the sod front. Mother
says idleness is the devil's workshop. Even though it is summer she
has set me to learn four-syllable words: consecutive/longevity/
sentimental/benefactor/incorporate/investigate.*

"There's just enough blue sky yonder for a pair of Dutchman's britches." Aunt Ida's prediction the next morning meant that only a stingy Dutchman could sew pants from the tiny patch of blue sky, but it also meant the day would clear. Aunt Ida went on, "I was out with my spade while you were away. It'll soon be time to start on the garden out back. That was a big one in its day."

Ma was serving coffee, eggs, and fried bread. She didn't respond, so Aunt Ida prodded. "What do you reckon to plant, Martha? That garden ain't been worked in so many years, the weeds will grow so big we won't even have to bend to grub them out." She poked Martin's shoulder with a finger as hard as an oak clothespin. "But that soil has been worked. You can always tell soil that was once worked. We'll have plenty for us, maybe even vegetables to sell in town."

Silently, Ma took her seat at the table.

"The garden is something we can do ourselves," Aunt Ida continued. "Even without Jacob's help. We'll do a huge garden right well before he ever gets back."

On and on she talked. Then, as clearly as warm breath vanishes in cold air, Martin's annoyance with Aunt Ida evaporated. He realized what she was doing. Elderly and frail as she was, she was trying to hold together their fractured family any way she could.

Ma studied the inside of her coffee cup, then poured one of her patent medicines into it. No one questioned Martin when he lifted the lunch pail off the dry sink and said good-bye, as if this were a usual morning.

He was tempted to ride Finn but had no intention of going to school and didn't want to draw his mother's attention to that fact. Not yet. He left on foot and followed the road to Perry's rail fence, then cut through the fields.

Mr. Perry answered his porch door, then stood far back as if welcoming Martin inside were an everyday occurrence. "Come in, boy, come in. You've come to tell me about Jacob. Sit down, sit down."

The house consisted of one large square room with a central stove and bedrooms off the far end. Mr. Perry poured steaming coffee into noisy tin cups. There were three chairs around the table and Martin wondered if he were sitting in the chair that Pa used growing up. "Pa's fine," he felt obliged to say, though that wasn't the reason why he had come.

"Well, go on, boy," Mr. Perry urged.

"He can't be moved for a while or even get up. They're taking pretty good care of him at the camp."

"Sounds like Jacob will be fine then. That's a relief."

Martin filled him in on the plan to bring Ma as soon as Pa could travel. "But that's not the only reason I came," Martin said.

"Oh?"

"I need to know what to do."

Mr. Perry looked confused.

"It's spring. Can you tell me what to do at the farm? What crops to get planted? Everything?"

"Whoa. So . . . you're planning to do it all yourself?" Mr. Perry eyed him. "If you'd been born to it, I might say you're almost ready to do a man's work."

"I can learn."

"Farming's like any job. It takes both knowledge and desire. I can see you're short on one and long on the other." Mr. Perry studied him. "With my health I reckon I can't be of much help except talking." He took more coffee and dropped a huge slug of sugar into his cup. "So we might as well get started. There's an old stone boat over on your place, still in pretty good condition. I saw it last year. It's a sledge for hauling rocks off the fields." A flash of worry crossed the old man's face. "It won't do to just put traces on it though. I'll loan you a chain and you'll use it, never mind the accident."

"I have Pa's tools—some slip hooks and grab hooks. He taught me sense around horses; I won't try to get them to pull too much."

Mr. Perry nodded his approval. "Some of your fields haven't been used in a while. Should grow good. Clean off the rocks, and you'll do all right. The plow for that place is in my barn. It's in good condition. Your horses will do fine with that plow. After plowing you'll do it all again with the spike tooth harrow to break up the chunks and snag out roots." He studied Martin's shoulders. "Only problem is a boy your size can't hardly manage rocks alone."

"I'll get help."

"Your pa won't like your ma doing such work."

"Not Ma, no. I have a friend from school," Martin said, thinking of Samson. It wasn't really a lie since Samson was a friend, sort of. Wherever he was. And they had met on a day he *should* have been in school.

Mr. Perry raised an eyebrow. "What boy around here isn't gonna be busy with his own place?"

"He's a visiting boy. Just visiting, doesn't have a place near here and really wants the work."

"Get those stones out now, and you'll be plowing soon enough. It's a mighty late spring so far." Mr. Perry sweetened the last of the coffee. "And your ma, what does she think of you handling the farm by yourself?"

Martin looked around the room, searching for a way to answer. "It's just till Pa gets back," he said. Useful items—rug beater, ladles, a coffee grinder—hung on the walls. His eyes fixed on the only decorative piece in the house, a painting.

"That picture there is your place." Mr. Perry pointed with

his sugar spoon. "The Gunnarsson homestead. Let's see . . . that was painted the summer before . . . before Cora and Jacob's mother died. Would you like to bring the painting home to your ma?"

"Another day, not today." Again Martin almost told Mr. Perry about Cora's diary, but it didn't seem right. Even Pa still didn't know.

Moving closer, Martin touched the canvas. Dried brush lines left ridges in the paint. "I can see the likeness now. The place looks different, though." The house logs were not yet covered with drop siding. Martin was seeing the place with dove-tailed corners where the squared-off logs of intersecting walls had been expertly fitted to each other. Like today, the barn was much larger than the house. The long garden showed behind and slightly to the side of the house; its windbreak of miniature evergreens was newly planted at the far end. Martin traced them with his finger. "These are huge now."

Mr. Perry came up behind him. "We brought the picture here for Jacob, so he could remember his roots. Some of these buildings aren't there anymore. 'Course, the barn's the same. This here was a chicken coop. And here was the springhouse. No one kept up the garden, and these honeysuckle bushes out front went wild. Your grandma Anna Gunnarsson had everything fancied up nice in those days."

Martin put his hand on a tall, heavily leafed elm tree that towered over all the structures. The bottom of the trunk divided into huge roots that buried themselves in the ground. "It's my chopping stump," he said, amazed.

"Fell down eight or ten years ago in a storm," Mr. Perry said.

Martin was seeing the exact world that Cora described in her diary. He had read so many passages about her doll's house and looked for it all over the farm. He had to know. "Mr. Perry, did my Aunt Cora have a doll's house?"

"Why, I don't rightly recall. Not that I would know of."

Mr. Perry smiled. "Say, that would be nice now for your sister, wouldn't it?"

Martin hadn't been thinking about Lilly, but he saw no reason to explain. He finished studying the picture, painted from the hillside in the common practice that Aunt Ida had described. He thanked Mr. Perry for the coffee and said, "I'll be back this morning with the horses to pick up the plow and chain."

17 October 1864

We are home from living in with the Connors. We waited there
two weeks for Ma's baby to come. The baby is a boy. He came in
the night, just like Ole Berg. Babies come at night. Father picked
his name before he left for the war. His name is Jacob. I did not
bring my volume, so there is much to record about those weeks.
Mother was pale blue for eight days after Jacob came. Blue
white, not pale like pink. I spent much time sitting by her bed.
I read aloud from the Bible or pieced my quilt squares. I have
four squares ready to change off with friends. I sat many hours
by Mr. Connor who knows carpentry like Father. My favorite
thing is the smell of freshly sawed wood. It is different from cured
firewood, which has lost its scent. I asked Ma if this is what roses
smell like. She said roses are even better. I gathered the pine curls
when Mr. Connor planed and called it a basket of rose petals.

—Cora Louise Gunnarsson, daughter and sister

Martin strode across the field, hopped the rail fence, and headed home without seeing that someone was following him. In his mind he worked out various ways to handle the coming encounter with Aunt Ida and Ma. It would be obvious right off that he hadn't gone to school, and he would have to explain his plans before taking the horses out.

A shower of small rocks landed around him. Martin's heart lurched. The Barkers. He balled his fists and turned.

"I'd about given up on you, boy." Samson was grinning.

Relief swept over Martin. But it's a universal fact that frightened boys must act tough, so he said gruffly, "How long you been following me?"

"Saw you going to that farmhouse. I waited while you were inside. What did you do in there anyway?"

"Why didn't I see you?"

"I'm magic!"

It was good to see Sam again. Even this odd Gypsy boy was better than having no friends at all. He kept walking, but backward, facing Sam, who trotted to catch up. "I thought you were going to watch for me in the afternoons."

Sam nodded. "I was gone with some of the men a while, but I've been watching this week for you and figured you were sick or skipping school."

"My pa had an accident at the logging camp. He broke his leg and can't be moved until after planting season. I went to see him and brought home our team."

They stopped, eye to eye. Martin read a message of sympathy in Samson's large brown eyes. "So I'm running the farm myself. Starting now, picking rocks." He didn't want anyone's pity. "I've got no time for fishing or carrying on."

He spun and continued walking. Sam followed, caught up, and matched Martin's gait. "I could help you," he said. "I want to be a farmer, and the plan is for us to camp the summer here."

"What do you know about farming?" Martin shot back.

Samson's face tightened to hide a smile. "About as much as you."

They had almost crested the hill in front of the homestead when Martin stopped and faced him. "I could use your help," he said, looking around as if words lay on the dirt road. "But . . ."

Samson finished for him. "You don't want your family to know about me."

Martin looked him square in the eye again and saw understanding. "I already have enough to explain today." He led Sam back around the hill so they could approach the barn from behind.

"Wait in here while I talk to my ma. She doesn't know yet about my quitting school or anything. I need to talk to her, then get back to Perry's for equipment."

As he approached the front porch door, Martin saw Aunt Ida in the garden, poking around with her spade. Inside, Ma stood behind Lilly's chair, removing thin white rags that had been tied in her hair the night before. She wrapped each yellow ringlet around her index finger before releasing it to fall in a tight coil. Ma looked so preoccupied with her thoughts that she didn't even register surprise when Martin walked in the door.

"Ma, I didn't go to school today. I went to see Mr. Perry."

Ma held a comb in her mouth. Her finger was wrapped with hair, and the ever-present tonic sat on the sideboard.

Martin crossed the room and poured coffee at the stove. "I told him about Pa, of course. But also I needed his advice about the farm."

Lilly winced as Ma pulled another knotted rag out. Ma asked, "What kind of advice?"

"Farming advice. What to do right off to get the crops planted." His mother blinked and refocused her gaze on him. "For Pa. I want to keep things going for Pa."

Ma patted Lilly's finished head but didn't look at him when she said, "You're just a boy. You can't do everything yourself. We should sell and go back."

Just a boy? He already did the work of a hired hand. "Nobody wants to get off this farm more than I do. But not until Pa's had a chance to make a go of it."

Ma looked thin and weak. "Mr. Meehan says why gamble that our first crops will be any good? Sell while we can."

Martin struggled to keep from raising his voice. "I'm doing this for Pa, but you've got to help, too, Ma. You've got to be strong and stop taking all this medicine."

Ma looked desperately around the room as if to locate the beloved potion.

"Meehan is thinking only about what's best for him. Don't let him scare you off even trying. Now," Martin stomped to the door, "I'm taking the team to Perry's to pick up the plow."

29 October 1864

The house is lonely without Father. I do my work quickly so I can spend time in my doll's house where I do not expect to see him. The weather is turning. A group gathered today to raise us a proper barn. Two girls of ten and eleven years came with three young children, still babies. We were told to mind the small ones all day. It was such a delight to have friends visit, and the children were no bother. We all played in my doll's house, the little ones even napping there. Caroline and Evelyn and I sat in my little parlor and sewed quilt squares. We brought tea from the cabin.

CHAPTER

Samson had backed out the horses and both were standing in harness when Martin entered the barn. Samson talked softly to the gentle giants as he finished with the straps. "You can lead them out front," he said. "I figured you plan to use that wagon."

Martin almost commented on Samson's way with the large horses that didn't know him, but then he remembered that Gypsies were famed for their abilities with animals. He opened the barn doors and led the horses outside toward the wagon while Samson slipped quickly from the barn into the open wagon bed.

In Mr. Perry's barn, the boys were loading the equipment when he came in. An awkward silence wrapped them, and they paused in their work as Mr. Perry studied Sam. Martin could see it was impossible not to notice Sam's clothes, loose fitting and different. And his dark skin and black curls. Sam didn't look like anyone in this area; he wasn't fair like the Swedes, Norwegians, and Germans.

Still no one spoke. Martin worried how Mr. Perry would react to Sam's being a Gypsy. He knew how Aunt Ida would react. He'd seen Aunt Ida almost attack Mr. Stone the photographer.

It was Sam who broke the silence. In his best, practiced,

unaccented English, he said, "Hello. I'm Sam." He completely took Mr. Perry by surprise when he wiped his hand on his pants pocket and stepped forward. Mr. Perry shook the hand and studied Sam.

He knows. Martin could tell. Would Mr. Perry let a Gypsy boy cart off a wagonload of equipment? Mr. Perry finally dropped Sam's hand. "I'm Perry" was all he said in reply.

Then Martin realized that this was a man whose family had plucked a baby out of a field and raised him. Taken an orphan and made him part of a family. No questions asked. Not then or now.

"That's a heavy team," Mr. Perry said, leaving.

Sam nodded. "Yes sir."

"You boys be careful."

Samson rode in the wagon bed with the plow, which intrigued him. He fingered the heavy blade, thick with grease to keep it from rusting. "What's the big chain for?" he asked.

Martin turned on the wide seat and settled in to talk. "To haul the stone boat. That's what I've got to do first, clear rocks off a couple of fields."

"You'll need me for that. Do we start today?"

Martin shook his head at his new, overly eager friend. "It sounds to me like the worst job on earth; you must want to be a farmer in a bad way." Martin felt the horses shift against each other and lurch on the reins. He turned toward them, noting the set of their ears before his own detected the rhythmic tickety-tickety-tock-tock of a motor.

"Somebody's coming behind. Stay down."

Martin gathered the reins firmly, but the horses quickly settled. They must have become accustomed to motor-driven saws at the logging camp, and they were plodding evenly again by the time the vehicle pulled up beside them.

Dang, it was Meehan. Without turning his head, Martin hissed over his shoulder, "Stay down, you hear? I don't want to have to explain you."

He had never studied Meehan's automobile up close. But he had studied enough of them to know that Meehan wouldn't be able to see over the wagon's sideboards. From his high wagon seat he towered above the man who waved at him to stop.

"Morning boy. Ain't you out and back early though."

The scent of barber's tonic rose up from the automobile below. The motor clickety-clicked now, almost louder than when it was in motion. Martin said nothing.

"Been to town?"

"No."

Meehan caught sight of the long arched wooden handles of the walking plow and rose up in his seat. "You hauling something there, boy?"

"Plow is all."

"And just what are you aiming to do with a plow?"

"Plow," Martin said.

"Really? With your daddy gone, don't you beat all doing that by yourself? And you just a schoolboy." Meehan raised a parcel. "I've brought your ma a supply of her tinctures and the mail and the tax notice from the bank. There's no letter come for you, though. Nothing from your friends."

The horses took three tentative steps forward, then waited for a signal from their driver.

Meehan shaded his eyes with a white-brimmed hat. "What you need is help. I'll talk with your mama about it today. Might be I could hire some hands for her."

Martin willed himself not to speak his full mind. He'd been taught to respect adults. Staring at the road he said simply, "No, thank you. We don't need any hands."

"Maybe, maybe not. Could be your mama won't want to keep the place with your pa like he is. I'd best get going; your ma is expecting me." Meehan held up a round pasteboard hatbox, tied in twine, with holes punched in the top. "And I've brought a little beauty of a cat to the ladies out your way. Won't your darling sister like that though?"

Martin lifted the reins and the horses picked up their feet. But he held them back enough that Meehan could go up the road ahead of them. This time the ground was hard enough that the automobile could drive into the farmyard.

It was not wise to have Samson come up to the barn again, so Martin dropped him off. "Head straight over this hill and wait for me," he said. "I'll harness the stone boat; then we'll start by clearing the field back of that stand of trees." Samson lumbered down awkwardly. "I could see him," Samson said, "through the crack in the boards. He doesn't like you much."

"I'm not going to be buffaloed out by the likes of him; I'll show him I'm old enough to run this place. One of my grandpas was married at sixteen and that's not two years off for me. Walk on, Finn. Get up, Marshall."

When Martin pulled up, he saw Lilly hugging the kitty with the hand that didn't clutch her doll. Meehan held a satchel of papers that spilled when Lilly ran at him with out-stretched arms and hugged his legs. Lilly would be hugging Pa that way right now if circumstances weren't wired up all wrong.

Martin drove past the distracted group to the barn where he stowed the plow, unhitched the wagon, and attached the chain to the stone boat. The ends of two heavy planks were beveled in front to crudely skim the ground, resembling a sled without runners or wheels. Rough boards were bolted across them to form the bed. The horses dragged the heavy platform. As Martin led them out toward the back hills, he saw Meehan head into the house with Ma.

As the days lengthened, suppertime inched later. Martin was exhausted after his third twelve-hour day of clearing rocks, each at least as heavy as a blacksmith's anvil. Even so, he enjoyed the sense of accomplishment that came with seeing the field clear and the rock piles grow. The farm felt less lonely too, probably because the horses were back. And he had to admit Samson was a mighty help on the pry bar used to move the rocks. Occasionally the boys took water breaks, and Martin would read the newspapers Mr. Perry passed along. Sam, who was quickly learning to read, loved sounding out the headlines.

"March is month date?"

"March is still news to us but too old to do anything about it," Martin said, leaning back.

"Who is Jack the Ripper?"

Pantomiming he held a knife, Martin explained about the discovery that George Chapman had murdered many women in London. He poked at a different article, "Read that instead."

"Thee bas-ee-ball rules com . . ."

"The baseball rules committee chairman proclaims—"

Sam nodded, "—that the pit-cher's box must not be more than 15 inches higher than the baselines or home plate."

"That's good. That's real good reading."

"What is this home plate?"

"Baseball? Someone hurls a ball and someone else hits it." Martin jumped to his feet, selected a clod of earth to toss skyward, then thwacked it with a branch as it fell. "It takes a lot of people, but you and I could practice hitting the ball."

Martin left the barn at dusk after bedding down the horses and nearly stepped on Lilly, sitting on a pile of fine sand and rubbing the blackened bottoms of the iron cooking pots to clean them. She was talking, as usual, to her doll. As usual, he ignored her.

Aunt Ida, who had waged a recent campaign to give Lilly more work to do, called from the house, "And you carry those pots inside too, you hear?"

Except for saying grace, the burden of mealtime conversation usually fell to the Gunnarsson women.

Aunt Ida said, "Better finish up that letter to your Pa, young lady. So it's ready to post next time Mr. Meehan passes by."

Lilly beamed. "Mr. Meehan is nice. He brought me Jack, my kitty."

"Now that I can get to town, I'll post our own letters," Martin said, taking a chunk of bread. "I can't see that we have much business for Meehan to concern himself with."

Ma said, "It was nice though that he made the trip to drop off the tax bill. And he brought an offer to buy the farm."

Martin's eyebrows shot up. He reminded himself to chew the mouthful of meat that almost went down whole.

"It was just a proposal to read and think over." Ma didn't look at Martin but busied herself cutting food on Lilly's plate. "Of course I would discuss it with Jacob before signing anything."

Aunt Ida finally put her oar in. "There's no sense in borrowing tomorrow's troubles. We're here now. And it's soon planting time. We'll all be busy, even you, young lady. Finish up now and fetch water to fill the reservoir."

That evening before going to sleep, Martin allowed himself to read one more of Cora's diary entries. He was nearing the end and trying to savor each one.

27 February 1865

Father got home last night. I don't know a word to say how happy we are plus how worried we are at his changes. He is so thin. He says the soldiers are sick and there are no provisions for feeding such large armies. He is well pleased with Jacob. I think Jacob has grown a lot because I know the months of work that have gone into that boy, but Father thinks Jacob is so small. Mother says to let Father alone, that he must sit many weeks by the fire to warm up. Ma is thin again, but looks like her normal self, not like Father. The wedding ring fits back on her finger.

—Miss Gunnarsson, schoolteacher

15 March 1865

I could not write until now. Pa died two days ago. The fever broke right before he died and Ma kept saying how sorry she was about a dowry. I did not understand many things she said. The Perry men fetched the Connors, but they did not arrive until late last night. Mr. Connor brings with him the smell of sawed pine again. The casket does not smell like roses to me now. There is still frost in the ground, but the men think they can get the grave dug. Mrs. Perry told Ma, "That's a blessing, no waiting." It didn't make me feel better. Nothing in the world will ever make me happy or lucky again. People say things to Mother like "It's not surprising, as sick as he was." But I am surprised. Death is a bad surprise, not like new babies. The ladies dressed Pa in his best clothes.

22 March 1865

"He whom the gods love dies young," wrote Menander, a Greek poet, who drowned. This the reverend said at the funeral, though he arrived three days after the burial. The days are like cheese with plenty of eyes. We wander through the house, Mother and me, discovering new holes everywhere. Many things want doing but this is a much harder grief than when Father was just away at war. Now the churn is idle, the cow cries out in newfound pain, even the smells are missing—of fresh dried washings and favorite foods.

CHAPTER

15

For six full days the boys crisscrossed two fields, picking stones and hauling them to corner discard piles. The ground was weedy and matted; the rocks were knitted into the dry earth's surface. They pried large boulders with the long iron rod Martin had found in the barn. In some cases removing a rock left a hole so deep they shoveled clumps of sod into it so the horses wouldn't stumble when they came back to work the field. They diligently removed all visible stones and hoped that more didn't lurk just below the surface, waiting to strike the plow blade.

Martin made an offhand remark that next year the rock clearing might not take so long, that he might need only one horse on the stone boat. He saw Sam's ears actually lower as his eyes bulged like wagon wheels. Sam jumped up and yelled, "YOU MEAN YOU HAVE TO DO THIS AGAIN?" The entire time it took Martin to explain about annual frost heave, Sam shook his head as if the sheer force of his will could prevent it.

They made a game of the tedious work by naming the larger stones they hauled—Reverend Rock, Straight Stone, Boring Boulder. One huge boulder remained; Martin hoped to bury it. The process involved digging a deep hole right next to it, so deep that the boulder could be pushed and pulled into it and then buried beneath a plowable depth of earth. Martin shared stories his father had told of farmers who had died or broken their legs attempting to bury rocks.

Sam's solution was to leave it in the middle of the field and name it Lunch Rock.

One morning Sam was not waiting in the field when Martin arrived. Martin had filled the stone boat twice before the heavy boy came staggering along, breathless and holding his generous middle.

He raised one hand to his chest, "Sorry I'm late today, Martin." Sam waded through rough grass to the stone boat.

"I went to town last night with my uncle. He had horses to sell, and I did magic tricks on the boardwalk." He helped Martin pick up rocks off the stone boat and together they hurled them at the pile of discarded stones. "I saw that fellow from the automobile, the one that came to see your ma. He was talking to a man about business things. . . . Sometimes folks talk right in front of us, like we're only there to entertain them. They figure we don't know anyone in the community, or maybe they think none of us speak English."

They chunked the rocks onto the heap. "He was talking about you, out here trying to farm alone. The man asked him if he still wanted your place. That Meehan fellow said yes, said the upgraded county road proposal goes right past here, and the hill your house is on will be the best site in the entire county for his big new home." The horses walked back into the half-cleared, half-rocky field without anyone directing them where to go. Martin waited, holding his heavy leather work gloves, until Samson had told him everything.

Martin resolved to see that Meehan didn't get his dream. His family would never stand in their own yard watching everything sold around them just for Meehan to have a new country house. Martin said, "It's nice to know his real reasons, Sam. I was thinking he might know something I don't. And I guess he does, but there's something else too." He weighed his secret and felt safe sharing a bit of it—not the diary-reading part, but the rumor. He explained about his grandmother coming to America with something mysterious, then entertained Sam with a recounting of every place on the homestead he had searched. Sam laughed at the image of Martin holding a lantern and peering down the privy hole.

During the days of hard work, the boys found four rattle-snake rattles, seven perfect stone arrowheads, and a spear-head. Martin attached a small canvas bag to Finn's harness to hold the treasures. Samson stooped, picked up a large chiseled point, and showed it to Martin. He dusted it as he turned it in the sunlight. Martin stopped picking rocks to admire the trophy and then watched as Samson passed his left hand over the point held by his right. The arrowhead disappeared. Samson grinned, and Martin had to admit he had a definite flourish.

"It's a good trick," Martin said, genuinely wondering at the stone's whereabouts since Samson wore a summer shirt with sleeves that ended above the elbow. The Gypsy smiled his toothy smile and showed both bare palms to Martin, then leaned to pet Finn high on the forehead and pulled the arrowhead from behind his twitching ear.

They worked until the sun was high and its hot rays followed them and stuck to their skin wherever they went. In seventy-two hours spring warmed from cool to planting weather; Martin could feel it in his bones. It was a Wednesday in late April when he and Samson finished picking rocks for the season. They would dump this one last load, then visit Mr. Perry. Martin needed more advice.

Samson spotted Lilly and pointed to her when she was still a field's width away. She walked slowly through the thick grass, her bonneted head dipping whenever she bent to pick a wildflower. Martin straightened, wiped his brow, and replaced his hat. He couldn't figure what Lilly was doing out here, and it annoyed him to have to stop and bother about her. There was no point in hiding Samson since she'd probably seen him already. He jerked his head toward the edge of the barren field. "My little sister."

"What's her name?"

Martin was surprised he would care to know. "Lilly."

She arrived at the rock pile and stopped to play. Martin ignored her until the stone boat was fully loaded. When they drove the load over, she was engaged in some game involving many tiers of flat rocks piled in front of her.

Martin did not greet her. It was Samson who approached first. "Hello, Lilly?" She looked up at him. "I'm Sam, Martin's friend. Have you come to visit us today?"

Lilly's curls jostled when she nodded. She stood and brushed off her skirt, then walked over to where a basket lay next to an armful of spring flowers. "Aunt Ida made me come. It's Ma's fresh bread and buttermilk."

Samson accepted the basket from the girl, studying her tiny pale hands. He rummaged under the napkin. "And butter too?"

"I made that. Aunt Ida says I must work more, or I will become a devil's workshop."

Samson laughed. Martin approached the two, explored the contents of the basket, then held it up. "Come on, there's plenty for two."

"And Lilly?"

"She can go back to the house and eat."

Samson didn't follow right away. He squatted and looked into the child's face. Kindly, he said, "Show me what you were playing over there."

Lilly smiled at Samson and bounced happily. She stopped before the pyramid of flat stones. Long braided strands of wild grasses flowed out and down the structure's sides from the various tiers of rocks that anchored them. Flowers were tucked into this rope, making the triangular pile quite attractive.

"It's *spitz kaka*," she announced, clasping her hands in front of her dress.

"What is this spits . . . what?"

"Wedding cake," she whispered from behind her hand as if Samson should be embarrassed for not knowing.

"It's lovely," he said. To Lilly's apparent surprise, Samson patted her on the head. "I wish I could eat it, but I have to content myself with plain bread today."

The boys had finished clearing Lunch Rock field and now rested and ate at the end of a long rock pile. That morning Martin had hauled out water for the horses on the empty stone boat; Samson left the lunch spot to see to watering them. Lilly knelt before her slab wedding cake, humming and prattling to herself.

Martin stared across the field they had labored to clear. His back ached from stooping and lifting but even more from the difficult labor of prying the rocks from the earth in which they seemed rooted. His eyelids were floating down in sleep when, half consciously, he noticed how quiet everything had become.

Aware that Lilly had been playing and singing on the ground to his side, he turned and studied her face, then followed her gaze. She strained to keep her snow-white features from trembling as she stared at a coiled rattlesnake, level with her neck. She still held a flower-decorated rock with both hands, and Martin could see that its weight would soon cause her to drop it.

Approaching from Lilly's other side, Samson whispered a Romany word, one of the few that Martin had learned. *Drab-aneysapa.* Poisonous snake.

As if angry at being interrupted from his noon nap, the agitated rattler danced from right to left. Then it concentrated on Lilly and grew motionless. It rose on its tail-like trunk and hovered in midair, without quivering. At the instant the serpent struck out at the tiny girl, a flash of red crossed its path. The snake's head bit and snagged on the offending fabric. Immediately a crash broke the silence and Lilly fell backward. Samson scooped her up and carried her toward the horses while Martin hit the snake three more times with the iron pry rod.

Lilly shook in Samson's arms. Her lower lip trembled, but she made no sound. He held her as Martin approached, holding up a red silk sash.

"We work well together," Samson said.

"Another trick of yours?" Martin asked shaking his head, his heart pounding. "I don't know where you hid this, Samson; you don't even have long sleeves on that shirt." Martin focused on Lilly then and borrowed a term of Aunt Ida's, "And you, young lady, don't you know these rock piles are filled with snake nests? You could have been killed. Even if it's not poisonous, snakes still bite and it still hurts."

Samson held up a hand to silence him. "Your sister has experienced . . . what is the word . . . a terror. This is not a good time to teach her anything." He turned and spoke soothingly to the child.

Teach? Martin had no intention of teaching her a lesson. He wanted to punish her for wasting daylight with her foolish notions about playing. Everything was always play for Lilly. He forced himself to step back and just breathe. No, it wasn't anger he felt; it was the realization that *Lilly could have died.* Martin's lunch squeezed up his throat as he imagined being responsible for another death.

But Lilly had already forgotten the fright. Samson had seated Lilly in the center of the stone boat and was entertaining her by walking on his hands. The muscles on his arms bulged under his considerable weight as he strained to lower his face so that he could pick a flower from the dirt with his teeth. He collapsed, tucked his head, and managed to roll onto his feet. Lilly rocked and clapped. Samson thrilled her, just like his brother, Dan, had done with his endless teasing.

Martin stooped to look in her face. He hadn't seen her this close up in a long time. "Listen, Lilly," he said sternly, "Ma and Aunt Ida don't know about Sam, and they can't know."

"How come?"

Samson joined them, pulled an arrowhead out of Lilly's ear, and brandished it. "Because I am magic, and if the grown-ups learn about me, I will disappear. Would you want that?"

Wide-eyed, Lilly shook her head until her curls wiggled.

"Then we have a deal?"

She solemnly shook Sam's hand.

As Lilly returned to the house with the empty lunch basket, Samson asked, "She is your only sister?"

"Yes."

"And no brothers?"

"I had one. Dan. He died in an accident." Then Martin told him everything. He described Dan, and Stillwater, and how hemmed in he felt despite the openness of this huge farm. It seemed easier to talk to someone who maybe didn't catch each and every word. Martin explained how mourning had put Ma off in her head, and to his surprise saying these things didn't make him feel worse. Grief had hollowed him out like a dried gourd, regret rattling in him like seeds. But by sharing, even a little, he felt as if the load of his memories was lightened by half.

Heading home, Lilly stopped fifty feet off in the field just to twirl, her face raised to the sun, arms outstretched. Martin thought about yelling a warning, *Open your eyes, there's holes, we cleared there.* But Sam, who also knew the dangers, just leaned on his shovel, watching and grinning.

Lilly's laughter reached them now. How Dan had loved to make Lilly laugh. The unforgiving sun burned the twirling image onto Martin's mind like a photographer's glass plate. Similar images crowded in of Lilly when she was three or four years old raising her arms to the boys—either boy—and saying "I need spinning!"

He remembered that once *he* also delighted in making Lilly laugh; *he* had swung her in great circles and teased her for sport. Maybe Martin had rewritten their history and convinced himself that Dan was the only brother she wanted.

Lilly dropped to the ground. Even Martin for all his watchfulness recognized it as joyous exhaustion.

"You protective her," Sam said.

"I am protective of her," Martin corrected, then thought *mind reader*. I have protected her. Even from myself.

That night Martin searched the homestead again. Sam's information about Mr. Meehan, coupled with the diary references, made him redouble his efforts. He scrutinized the remains of the dilapidated shed and the sod stable his grandparents had used before building the barn. He recalled every tiny building from the homestead painting at the Perrys'. Had Cora used the springhouse as a play place? The windmill took its place now, but he poked around the footings anyway with a shovel. He reexamined some of Cora's diary entries about her doll's house and investigated every inch of the homestead as it would have been in her day. Under the guise of dismantling it, he explored the ruined chicken coop. Certainly no child had played dolls in a messy chicken coop. He sighed. Maybe Mr. Perry was right. And Pa. Maybe it was just a rumor.

5 April 1865

Jacob is bringing us back to our normal selves. Even Mother. A baby gives love, but a baby also brings work that has to be done. Last night Mother spoke about her life in Sweden. I think that I will never see my grandfather who lives there. In Sweden there is not much land like in America. Swedish farms always go to the sons—and maybe just to one son, the oldest. She talked to me in whispers even though we could shout here and no one would ever hear us. My grandfather gave land to his sons and a dowry to my mother. I don't know exactly what this means. Mother says we will try to finish proving up our homestead, which means we have to live here three more years. But if we can't we will be safe. She wants me to understand the family plans now and not to worry.

"*G rai,* horse." Samson pointed at Finn. During lunch breaks he taught Martin Romany words. *"Kanni,"* Samson waved the thighbone he was eating.

Martin said, "Chicken?" Then when Sam held up bread, "Don't tell me, ahh ... *panum.* How do you say 'ants'?"

"Emets."

"How do you say 'automobile'?"

Sam turned his serious teacher face to Martin and enunciated slowly, "Au-to-mo-bile." Both boys laughed.

They also exchanged lunches most days. Martin liked the spicy Gypsy fare, and Samson marveled at Swedish breads and sweets, though despite eating Martin's generous lunches, Samson was getting thinner and stronger.

Unsealing the earth was more difficult than Martin ever imagined. They traded off Finn and Marshall so each horse pulled the plow half a day. It was hard work holding the hand plow steady and straight, while at the same time keeping the blade a uniform depth underground. Their first plowed furrows were so uneven that Samson laughed and said, "I told you that Roma can't farm!"

The new work accentuated the horses' personalities. Taking to farming, Finn pulled evenly. The beast sensed when the plowshare was surfacing and would slow a bit so Sam or

Martin could dig in hard with the handles. Marshall acted like fieldwork was beneath him. Although he skidded logs on ice roads all winter, he was soiling his hooves now. The boys could make him obey, but they started to call him Mister Marshall when he got too contrary.

Spending long days together they had also grown comfortable with silence. Almost like friends. Almost like when Martin would sit quietly fishing with Stan and Chet. At times he and Sam talked, moving from discussions about farmwork to talk about their lives. Each wanting the life the other had.

They shared bits about themselves, but both also held back certain information. Sam shared that his parents had died of influenza—he remembered them only vaguely—but despite Martin's questions, Sam wouldn't talk about Ruby other than to say she was his cousin.

Martin did not tell Sam that he was reading his aunt's childhood diary, but day by day he shared more about his brother. He tried to explain how Dan *was,* about how people liked him the best, even Lilly. How Martin always had to be the serious one, the one to remember instructions, to stick to the job at hand because Dan was always testing and doing daring things.

Sam said nothing, but Martin could feel that he was listening. They had stopped for lunch and in no time an hour had gone by.

"Dan bragged; he always bragged."

Sam looked puzzled, so Martin swaggered his shoulders and explained, "Brag means saying you can do anything. Dan was wild-eyed; he bragged he could go right under that horse's belly on his damn sled. I couldn't stop him. . . . That's how he died." Martin put a gloved hand to his throat. "Do you know that word? Decapitated?"

"Not till now." Sam leaned on the plow, pulling long grass between his fingers and listening.

"My mother doesn't know that. Not everything. Pa told her Dan looked so peaceful—like he was sleeping—that she should remember him that way and not come to the undertaker's. Everyone let her think he just hit a tree or a rock or something. My parents spent everything they had on his funeral. Everything. That funeral was a scam."

Sam pointed across the rocky field. "Look. There. A man is coming." He slipped from behind the plow into the woods behind the rock pile. Martin cleaned up their lunches and started Finn back into the field. It was Meehan.

Martin could see him clearly now. Meehan picked his way, head bent, across the rutty ground. He had no hat, and mopped his brow with a handkerchief, then stopped and lifted each foot to wipe dirt from his shoes. Martin steered Finn away from the Lunch Rock and farther up the windbreak.

"Ain't you something there, boy? Out here working by yourself. What's that you're doing?"

Martin remembered what Sam had said. He didn't like that Meehan had been talking about their farm in town. Feeling cautious, he decided not to give much information. "Plowing."

"Why, look there." Meehan pointed ahead to a low fence that boxed in a square of earth near the edge of the woods.

It was the Gunnarsson family gravesite.

Meehan waved at the spot. "You don't see these places much anymore, now there's a proper cemetery in town."

Martin fought to keep his tone respectful. "What brings you out here, Mr. Meehan?"

Meehan held up his hands to imply nothing, nothing at all. "I was just going past and thought I'd look the place over good."

"For what?"

"Well, it's a fact that your pa hasn't sent money since that accident of his. Taxes will come due. I'm just seeing what all this farm consists of in case you folks decide to sell. It's for your family's own good."

Why did Ma tolerate this man coming around? Since

Dan's death she was so passive. Martin remembered the Ma who once would have dismissed the likes of Meehan. Was he old enough to stand up to Meehan? How old was old enough?

"No thanks." Martin started Finn walking. "Mr. Perry told me how you tried to buy him out, too. Was that for his own good?"

"Boy, there's no fool like an old fool, and Perry's an old fool. He should move to town if he can't handle farmwork."

Martin didn't feel like a boy. He was only fourteen, but fourteen and in charge of a farm, an elderly great-aunt, sick mother, and little sister. He decided right there that fourteen was old enough to speak back. He wouldn't tell Meehan off, but he could surely dismiss the man.

"I'm burning daylight. Good-bye." Martin grappled with the plow handles.

Meehan, choosing each step carefully, couldn't keep up when Finn stepped out smartly.

He called after Martin, "Foreclosure is an awful business that takes a long time. You think about it. My way would get you folks some money at least."

"Whoa." Martin turned. "For today, and whether I like it or not, my family owns this place. As far as I'm concerned, Mr. Meehan, you're trespassing."

"You won't dare be so high-and-mighty disrespectful when I come here with foreclosure papers."

"No. Don't. Don't *you* bring the papers. When it's time for those papers, send someone else."

By the time Martin returned to where Sam hid in the woods, he felt an odd sense of power, almost relief.

"What did he want?" Sam inquired.

"Meehan? Up to his usual no good."

"What did you tell him?"

Martin grinned, "I told him *'jal avree!'*" Go away. "That magic of yours works good, Sam."

B it by bit darkness fell later each night. Sunlight seeped into the earth and the ground softened. "It's time to plant corn when you can sit on the ground and it doesn't feel cold," Mr. Perry said. Martin had found him disassembling a harvester in the sunlight of his open barn doors. The man appeared red-nosed and miserable, his irritated eyes still so bloodshot they looked orange. "This here I used to harvest oats and small grain. That's the other thing, Martin." He stood to blow his nose. "You need to plant a field in oats and alfalfa. The oats are ready to cut and thrash by July; then the hay comes up for fall. You boys will do right well to get crops of corn, oats, and alfalfa."

The large man stepped out the barn door and spat generously onto a pile of soiled straw. "You'll be able to feed quite a few animals through next winter or sell the feed for cash. Whichever you decide. You're learning fast. Maybe next year you and your pa can manage my place, too. Someone's gotta work my land eventually."

According to Mr. Perry the disc harrow came next. Again Sam and Martin retraced their steps across the fields they had cleared and plowed; this time the horses pulled a contraption of sharp metal circles that broke up large clumps of earth.

Finally they had cleared and plowed, harrowed and

cross harrowed. Planting, when the time came at last, felt like not a chore but a reward. They created straight rows of corn planted exactly thirty-six inches apart and forming a series of squares across the field. The nearly perfect spacing between stalks and between rows would allow the cultivator to move between the young plants without damaging them.

With the plowing and planting done for the season, the boys no longer needed to see each other regularly. But Sam came often to the homestead through the pasture, carefully entering the barn from below. They continued the language lessons they'd shared during breaks on Lunch Rock. Sam was stymied by idioms, collected any he heard in town, and brought them to Martin to explain.

"To boot? A man at the stables asked me to throw in a bridle *to boot.* And what about *smell a rat* when there are no rats? I often hear this *barking up the wrong tree.*"

But his English was very good now. Martin only occasionally had to explain that receptable or progressful weren't words, or that instead of "in momentarily" Sam should say either "in a moment" or "momentarily."

One morning Martin found Sam feeding Finn and Marshall. The dark, once pudgy boy had changed dramatically from the heavy fieldwork. Muscle tone had replaced the soft flesh on his belly, and his forearms were hardened from steadying the plow.

Martin felt, for the first time in weeks, the odd sense of having time on his hands. "I started to worry Mr. Perry would never stop thinking up new reasons for us to walk over those fields." Martin patted the plow. "Today I'll plow the garden, then grease this and store it away."

Samson grinned at him. "You're starting to look dark, like me." He nodded at Martin's red, burned face and shoulders.

"Summer's here; that sun was almost hot yesterday."

When Samson smiled his teeth shone bright in his dark face. "I have the perfect way to celebrate the end of planting." He rubbed Finn's muzzle before feeding him. "Come to a wedding tonight."

"A wedding? Where?"

"At the meadow where we're camped. I came to invite you." Samson could barely contain his excitement. He ran his hands over the large animal's flank.

Not wanting to disappoint him, Martin said, "Well, now, I don't know."

"We'll be dancing and there'll be lots of music and food. Always is; could last till morning. Come late, after your people go to bed."

"I'll see," Martin managed. As he picked up the shovel to clean Marshall's stall, he thought back to his last visit to the Gypsy camp. His only visit. He remembered Ruby, who hadn't liked him much. He remembered liking her green eyes though. "I'll give it a try," he said as he flung the manure out of the barn.

Aunt Ida rummaged on the shelf to find her favorite glass for flattening cookies, a large flat-bottomed glass, not the small jelly glass she slipped into socks for darning. Martin watched her roll the dough between her palms, then place the balls on a baking tin. She dipped the glass in a saucer of sugar and flattened each cookie before baking.

"May I have the leftover sugar for a tea party?" Lilly asked when the cookies were in the oven.

This was the longest Martin had lingered in the kitchen in a month. It surprised him to see how little the women's lives had changed with the turn of the seasons. He had been so busy learning how to farm and accomplishing all the early spring chores that he hadn't noticed their routines were much the same. There was more contact with people, peddlers and such, now that the roads were open. And food from town was more plentiful with the horses and wagon for transportation, but otherwise they were still inside, cooking or ironing, like they had been in winter. He was glad he had time today to get the garden ready for them.

Ma came in from gathering eggs. Aunt Ida held out a hand for the basket. She'd already lit a candle and would hold each egg in front of the flame so she could see through the shell. "I need to candle those for custard. My recipe calls for double-yolk eggs."

Martha hung firmly onto the handle. Her voice carried today; it sounded lower and more controlled than usual. "I don't understand why you won't just separate some eggs and use extra yolks."

There was something different about Ma's voice. Martin glanced at Lilly, who was already looking at him. There was a touch of the old Ma in Ma's voice, the Ma who sometimes lost her temper because Aunt Ida was so set in her ways.

Aunt Ida let her stand there clutching the basket. She moved to the cookstove and turned a tray of cookies in the hot oven. She nodded in confirmation and said, "My recipe is certain—double-yolk eggs." The old woman smoothed the flour-sack apron over her tiny waist and continued in a voice that ignored the difference of opinion they had just shared. "Now, Martha, I looked at your garden plan."

She walked to the sideboard and straightened a sheet of drawing paper with her forearm. "This here won't do. You planned the sunflowers so they shade the carrots and beets." Aunt Ida began to sketch in changes with a pencil, boldly scratching changes to Ma's plan, almost daring Ma to object. "We'll do pole beans and cucumbers along here. And that's already hollyhocks and iris. No point in wasting God's time trying to move them." She pulled at one long sagging earlobe. "Martin, can you get some wire fence? We'll set it along here for peas to climb."

"I won't be going to town until it rains," he said automatically, before realizing he had the time to go now whenever he wanted.

"If you finish plowing the garden today, we'll plant tomorrow," Aunt Ida told him. "The wire can go in later."

Maneuvering in the garden space was much tighter than a field, but Martin was now proficient with the plow. The weather of the last two weeks had been warm but overcast and now gave way to searing sun and a hot afternoon. Lilly brought him lemonade and stayed to watch the turning over of the earth, her doll tucked under her arm.

While Martin harrowed the garden plot, Aunt Ida dug around the edges with her spade. She complained about the work, but Martin bet she looked forward to having a garden like she had as a girl. Ma hung sheets on the line—perfectly, carefully, loudly snapping tea towels and pillow linens.

Martin turned Finn in the confined space and saw Lilly's feet running under the full clotheslines. Washings were one thing Ma was still particular about. Martin remembered how, as children, he and Dan would run under the sheets as Lilly was now doing. They played hide-and-seek and let the sheets drape over them as they ran until Ma would shoo them away. Ma had hated it; she always shooed them away.

Lilly pulled too hard, and one sheet came off in her hand. Martin stepped out from behind the horse and would have called to her, but now Aunt Ida was watching, too, from the other end of the garden plot. They looked at each other, then watched as Lilly kept running and pulling at the wash behind Ma's back.

"Stop that!" Ma shouted when she turned and saw the sheet lying in the dirt. Martin and Aunt Ida stood frozen by the sound of Ma's voice—not a whisper. Ma was mad.

Lilly kept running and pulling. *She dropped her doll.* Lilly glanced at Martin, then Aunt Ida. When they did nothing, she looked Ma in the eye. She challenged Ma with her stare, but she kept pulling.

"Stop that *right now,* young lady." It was Ma's mad voice. Ma's "watch out" warning voice. It had been silent for a year.

Lilly jerked a bedsheet, and the wire line broke, dragging sixty feet of wash to the ground.

Ma lunged at her—the same Ma who could chase down her two small boys when they needed spanking. Ma grabbed Lilly by the apron, but Aunt Ida was suddenly there. Aunt Ida, who loved to say "Spare the rod and spoil the child," didn't say that today.

She stepped between them. "Martha, let's just send this young lady to the well for water. We'll have her rewash everything."

Ma was shaking mad.

But Lilly was mad too, mad from a year of sadness. Lilly stomped toward the pump, passing Ma's washstand. Out flashed her little hand. As fast as an ax cleaves kindling, she flipped the open bottle of patent medicine into the washtub of sudsy water.

Ma flew after her again, but this time Martin said, "Let her go, Ma. She's got the grit to make you come back when the rest of us do nothing but tiptoe around you." He had Ma's attention. "Lilly needs you. We all need you. Pa will need you more than ever. You never care about anything anymore. You're half asleep all the time from that medicine."

Ma stooped to pick up the soiled sheets. "It's been a hard year," she said in her passive voice again. Martin didn't know how to reply; Ma could have been referring to an uncommonly cold winter or a large snowfall. He watched, silent, while Ma searched for a clean spot on a damp sheet to catch the tears that started down her face.

Ma was crying.

Martin wanted to go to her, to say "That's good Ma, let it out." But Ma continued, "If only Dan didn't have to die."

"Have to die? He didn't have to die." Martin was surprised he spoke out loud. Were they going to talk about it now? In the garden, with the dirty sheets? But he couldn't stop. "Dan didn't *have* to die, any more than he *had* to always be reckless. He chose to be that way. It wasn't a tree, Ma. When Chet and I got to the sledding hill, we told him not to go down that side. We told him it was dangerous with the road below, with old man Kearney's dairy wagon at the bottom. But there was no stopping him."

At the house Lilly pumped water furiously. Aunt Ida inched her way closer over the plowed soil.

"Dan was *older*; he should have been the responsible one.

But Dan never listened to anybody. A boy on a sled is probably faster than a horse running flat out."

Aunt Ida gathered sheets off the ground, looking like she wasn't listening.

"Mr. Kearney pulled the wagon forward. I tried to stop him. I tried to stop the wagon. I hollered. I ran. But Mr. Kearney didn't hear me. You remember how deaf he was? Dan couldn't change the path he was on. The horses pulled the wagon box right in his path. His head . . ."

Ma's hands flew to her breast. Aunt Ida bent her head.

Martin paused. When he spoke again his tone was spent. "I'm through being responsible for Dan. Sure, Lilly liked him best. He was the fun brother." He shook his head, remembering. "When we'd go swimming, Dan would jump off dangerous cliffs while I'd watch Lilly on the shore. I still feel responsible for him, like it was my fault somehow."

Finn nickered softly, calling Martin back to the plow.

"I can't help feeling we're here because of him. But you know what? Dan would never do this for me. He'd never live the life I have on this farm."

Ma put a hand on Martin's cheek. They looked into each other's eyes, really looked. He decided to take responsibility for his brother one last time. "I know you blame me for Dan, that he died and I lived. That's the truth, isn't it?"

Ma's eyes, which hadn't been sharp or focused in a long time, widened in alarm. "No, Martin. No." She gripped his shoulders. "I see now my grief has been a selfish thing. I never blamed you. I blame myself. And God maybe." Ma dropped her hands and spoke to the ground. "I'm so sorry."

Martin shook his head. "I have wanted to go back to Stillwater so bad. But I've been missing friends who've never even written to me. Maybe all I've really been missing is our family, not a place. Maybe the place doesn't matter." Martin passed the harness through his hands, looking for a frayed section, then stretched it across the plowshare, severing it in half. "We're like a harness; we get broken, maybe even lose an entire section. But mending is an option. Never the same, but mended. Shorter maybe, but stronger. A harness rarely breaks in the same spot twice."

Ma squeezed her mouth and nodded.

"We need you, Ma." With his hand on her elbow Martin turned her around. "We need you to care about what goes in this garden, and to make us supper at night, and to take after Lilly when she disobeys."

"Oh, yes" was all Ma said, wiping her eyes and sniffing. They returned to their work in silence. A *good* silence. Aunt Ida helped Lilly turn sheets in the wash boiler while Ma re-attached the clothes wire. The warm air smelled of summer. Martin felt lighter, almost *normal*. He welcomed the work as he picked up the plow handles.

Martin was exhausted by the afternoon's events and another day of working in the sun. It had been so hot he'd removed his shirt just for an hour or two. Sitting in the kitchen after supper, he tried to scratch his back.

"Martin, your neck is burned. Sunburn is no different from any type of burn. I knew a baby once that died from it." Aunt Ida nodded gravely. "The mother left the baby in the sun all day, and he blistered right up. Treat it just like a fire burn, I always say."

She moved to the hutch where the coffee, flour, and supplies were kept in small usable portions and retrieved a jug of vinegar. Vinegar was Aunt Ida's solution to everything. Each Saturday night when Lilly bathed, Aunt Ida did the final rinse of her hair in vinegar. It usually took until Monday before the girl stopped smelling of the stuff.

Aunt Ida saved clean muslin scraps as bandages, and Martin always thought she looked slightly happy when some injury finally put them "to good use." She soaked a clean bandage in a bowl of vinegar, wrung it out, and spread the cool stinking cloth on his neck. She soaked others for both shoulders and handed him one to hold across the bridge of his nose.

He sat awhile and felt the heat go out of his burned skin. As his mood improved he seriously considered a late-night venture to the Gypsy camp.

"Best thing for you is to rest," Aunt Ida explained, removing the cloths. "My mother's remedy was olive oil. You sleep the night with this rubbed in good, and you'll be fine as frog's hair by morning." There was no stopping her when she knew a proven remedy. She rubbed the greenish-amber oil into Martin's back and shoulders.

Aunt Ida was gentle, and Martin knew this was her way to heal the necessary but fresh wounds of the afternoon's encounter with Ma. But now he smelled bad and felt greasy. There would be no chance to wash it off either, since he did his bathing here in the house, as Pa would say, "once a week whether we need it or not."

Aunt Ida went to the door and called Lilly. "With these long summer evenings starting, that girl doesn't get enough sleep," she said to no one in particular.

Martin stretched until his chair squeaked. "Well, that's not a problem for me. Good night." He went out to the barn and climbed to the loft to wait until the house grew quiet. He pulled out his calendar. Some weeks back he had stopped crossing out the days until his return to Stillwater and had begun a daily farm log of what he had plowed and harrowed and seeded. He made an entry for the garden and slowly fell asleep to the crickets, night owls, and sounds of the warm barn.

CHAPTER

Martin dozed and awoke in pain when he rolled onto a sunburned shoulder. Even the night insects were quiet. He couldn't find a comfortable position for sleeping and had no way of judging time. Maybe not yet midnight. He lit the lantern. There was only one entry left in Aunt Cora's diary—the very one he had skipped ahead to read first. That seemed so long ago now.

6 July 1865

Mother is sick. Not even Father was this sick. She told me to take Jacob to the Perrys. Her last words were about a dowry, which I hid safely in my doll's house. Jacob is starting to cry. I am afraid to disobey her, but I am also afraid to leave her alone.

Martin turned several pages, but there were no more entries. He lifted the book to his nose and breathed, but there was nothing more of Cora left, not even her scent. He knew that the writing stopped because Cora also died that day. He wished she could be his aunt now, that he could have known her in life. Then he realized he would know nothing of her at all if it weren't for this diary. It was her gift to him. As Martin extinguished the lamp, he resolved to share it with Pa one day. He pulled on his shirt and pants and decided to walk to the Gypsy meadow to see whether the wedding party was over.

The moon was even more full than the night before, so he had no trouble finding the path to the lake. The night air no longer held the chill of winter. From a half mile away he heard the music and saw the glow of many fires.

He stood at the edge of the clearing, trying to pick Samson out in the crowd. His first time here he had been struck by the colors of the place. Tonight, even by moonlight he made out bright cloths on tables everywhere. The wagons were bedecked with early spring flowers and ribbons. He walked cautiously toward the nearest fire.

Two men sat with their backs to a table and played small guitars. A group of dancers whirled around the open fire nearest them. Martin watched, mesmerized, as Ruby danced with a tiny boy of four or five. She wore a pumpkin-colored skirt and dark purple blouse. From her ears dangled golden hoops, larger than any earrings he had seen. Gold bracelets slid together, then apart, on her long forearms. Other women wore bracelets above their elbows, a custom Martin had never seen before.

Ruby stopped, still holding the boy's hand, when she spotted him. Others turned to follow her gaze until it seemed all heads turned in his direction, and people murmured *gadjo*. Ruby went between two wagons, called out in their strange tongue, and seconds later Samson came galloping around the collection of tables to greet him.

"Martin! I was beginning to think you couldn't get away. Come, come and sit here."

The music started again, and people slowly resumed their activities. Dogs, large and small, milled about the crowd. Everywhere soft lantern light glowed on tables.

"You missed the wedding," Samson said. "Was it hard to get away?"

"I fell asleep."

"I'm surprised you felt up to it, the way you look." He pointed to Martin's red face and neck. "Does it hurt?"

"Only if I move . . . or breathe or smile."

Samson laughed. "Grandmother knows you are here; she's bringing food."

Martin wanted to say he wasn't hungry, but just then Grandmother parted the crowd with a plate of food held high in each hand. A reluctant Ruby followed, carrying a pitcher and glasses. She placed them unceremoniously on the table next to Martin. Grandmother spoke a command, and Ruby picked up the glass and filled it.

Martin didn't miss the thump with which Ruby set the glass back on the table. "Thank you," he said, picking up the goblet and sipping the sweet homemade wine.

Grandmother placed the large platters of food in front of Martin and Samson. Then she stood with her short round arms crossed until Ruby warily sank into the chair opposite Martin.

The boys ate their homemade breads, desserts, and spicy chicken. Martin felt some of the eyes finally turn away from him. He hoped that talking about food was a safe topic.

"This is delicious chicken," Martin said.

"I chased it, and caught it, and wrung its neck." Ruby twisted her wrists.

Samson explained, "We believe that you have to catch chicken. The fastest are the most delicious."

Grandmother had retreated to a group of older people. Whenever she stared pointedly at Ruby, the girl would make a brief effort at conversation. For the most part, she sat with her back to Martin so that all three faced the dancers.

Martin studied her hair, left long, with only the sides caught back loosely in a clasp. The barrette was covered with fresh flowers. He was not accustomed to seeing women wear their hair down. Aunt Ida's was even longer, he knew, but he had seen it straight just once. Even Ma wore her hair up always.

"Well? Do you or don't you, Martin?" Samson called.

Martin turned a blank face to his friend.

"Do you want to dance with Ruby?"

Martin looked down at his empty plate. He'd never danced with a girl. He wanted to say "no," or would "no thanks" be better? But "ah, sure," came out of his mouth instead. He clumsily got up and went around the table.

Ruby moved into the gathering of dancers, and Martin followed, feeling as stiff as a fence post. She had left her shoes under her chair. As her bare feet caressed the cool earth, a gold bracelet flashed on one ankle. Ruby slid and swayed to the music, while Martin stared at her, wondering what to do. He had never once danced in his life, not like Lilly was always doing.

She studied him, then smiled a broad smile, as if she knew. She moved closer. "What were you dreaming about back there?"

He could hardly say he had been lost in thought about her hair. Martin searched the corners of his mind for any other answer, but none would come. She glided in front of him, swinging her full orange skirt, her earrings shimmering. "Maybe you were worried about being with Gypsies. We'll steal you blind, you know. We're no good. Your people call us vagrants."

Martin found his tongue, but still he stood stiffly, as if planted in the ground. "Not that at all. Samson is my friend."

"Because he works for you," she spoke louder now, swaying to the music in contrast to Martin's awkwardness.

"That's not it," Martin said.

"He works your land for free." Ruby fairly spit out the words.

Martin wondered what he had ever done to upset this girl and make her react so violently to him. She had agreed to dance with him only to get away from her grandmother and be free to insult him. How could just being a *gadjo* inspire such hatred? He made an effort to control his voice. "Samson is a true friend. I had work to do, and he wanted to help."

Martin saw Ruby catch a signal from Grandmother. She swallowed her ready reply and concentrated on gliding around him. Then, with a backward glance at Grandmother, she picked up Martin's frozen arms and placed them lightly on her shoulders, placing hers likewise on his shoulders.

She felt soft and firm at the same time. Ruby coaxed him into moving. He followed each of her slow steps. After two or three minutes that felt longer than all of last winter, she smiled at him, genuinely pleased. Without completely stopping, the music changed to a different tune. Martin looked around at the group of dancers. Most men held the women they danced with closer. He considered moving his hands to her waist, then thought better of it. He could tell without touching that Ruby wouldn't be stiff and hard like corseted women. They danced, slower than the others, in the middle of the crowd, their bodies coming closer and closer to one another as the music hypnotized them.

He was looking straight ahead and at the same time seeing her hair with his side vision. He had just about decided to brush her hair with his cheek when she fixed her green eyes on him and said, "What's that smell?"

He held her back a little and looked at her, a question on his face.

She leaned in closer and sniffed at his shirt. "Like laundry. Sometimes we put vinegar in the laundry; it gets out the smell of horses."

Martin stood still. He had never danced with a girl before, not even Ma. He had barely even talked to one, let alone held one in his arms. He didn't even know what to say to his sister most of the time. In his worst nightmares he had never dreamed that a girl would comment about his smell. There was nothing, not one experience in his entire lifetime, to see him through this moment. He felt a response well up inside him. For a second he feared he might cry. Then it came out, but as a great gust of laughter. Ruby looked at him for a time; then she laughed, too. Everyone else danced around them, but they stood, locked in an embrace, laughing. For the first time Ruby seemed to be comfortable with him, to like him.

"It's me," Martin managed to say. "My great-aunt, I mean my mother's aunt, lives with us and vinegar is her remedy for sunburn. For just about everything, really."

"Come," she said, and slipping his hand from her shoulder into her palm, she led him away from the fire. They were still laughing.

Ruby looked back at him shyly. "I told Grandmother when I saw you tonight that you looked like something freshly butchered. I have my own cure for that burn."

She led him to Grandmother's familiar wagon. "Sit," she told Martin, pointing to a log by a fire that was reduced to embers. Ruby lifted a jar from a tub of water and dried it off on her skirt. "It's buttermilk. We keep it cool in springwater. The buttermilk is an antidote to the color; it whitens the skin."

She went inside and returned with a soft scarf. They sat together at the fire. Ruby wrung the cloth in the cold milk and gave it to Martin, who held it on his face, neck, and shoulders. They talked easily for the first time, mostly about him and the farm and the difficult adjustment from city life.

Ruby listened to it all. She rinsed the cloth again, then drained the pan over the fire. "Sometimes the women use buttermilk to whiten their skin," she said to the fire. "I don't approve."

"You're lighter than many of the people here," Martin observed.

"It doesn't matter," she said hotly, a little of the former Ruby returning to her voice. Then she softened. "I suppose you think they stole me as a baby and that's why I have lighter hair and green eyes."

Martin was tired and had no fight left in him. He studied the night sky; the moon had traveled swiftly across the royal-blue darkness. He waited as a single black cloud crossed its path, robbed the moon of its light, and then slowly passed.

"To tell the truth, Ruby, my aunt is full of stories about Gypsies. She's filled my head with warnings since I can remember. You probably wouldn't like knowing that I've kept Sam a secret from my family."

Ruby said nothing in response to his honesty.

"The first day I followed Sam here, I thought I was in trouble for sure. Then I saw you're all just people, like anyone else."

They looked at each other in the amber glow of the small fire. "I don't remember ever laughing like that," he said. "My ribs hurt." Martin patted his chest, then stretched and rose. "I better be going."

They found Samson, and Martin thanked him for the invitation. The boy looked pleased at the sight of his friend and cousin getting along.

Ruby walked Martin to the edge of the clearing where his clothes had once hung drying. "I suppose I should thank you," he laughed. "Now I smell of olive oil, vinegar, and buttermilk."

She leaned into his shirt and breathed deeply of his scent, then spun on her bare heel and bounded back toward the fires.

CHAPTER

19

S eeds sat in the earth; their only moisture the memory of melted snow from last winter.

But Mr. Perry said that drought didn't pose a danger until the seeds germinated. Martin became preoccupied with watching for the crops to sprout, and so preoccupied with thoughts of Ruby—her hair, her laugh, her soft body when they were dancing—that he could barely perform routine tasks like milking Ella. One day he was checking Marshall's hooves when he realized he'd already been all the way around the horse and was picking up his feet for the second time.

A week after the wedding at the Gypsy camp, Martin decided he had the time to go into town. And just maybe he would run into a certain young lady with green eyes. Aunt Ida declared she had too much work to do with the garden and spring housecleaning. Ma didn't go either, but for the first time she didn't ask Martin to bring back medicines or remedies. Ma had even taken up sewing again. Not just mending or patching, she was making Lilly a new Sunday dress.

Lilly had no desire to stay behind with two women who would certainly try to best each other at giving her work. She opted for the long wagon trip, even if her brother would most likely make the journey without speaking to her.

In town Martin bought wire fencing, flour, and other

supplies. He posted Ma's letter to Pa and retrieved their mail, which consisted of an almanac, an issue of *Ladies' Home Journal,* and a letter from Pa to Lilly. Lilly laughed as she shook a nickel from the envelope. In the letter Pa sounded very encouraged and said he hoped to be able to make the journey home within three weeks.

Martin helped Lilly select penny candy; then they walked around town on the boardwalk, Lilly holding her doll in one hand and the sack of candy in the other. More people congregated in town on Saturday night than any other. Tonight everyone was attracted to a small gathering at the livery stable. Both he and Lilly were pleased to see that Samson and Grandmother were the center of attention. Martin searched the crowd for Ruby but saw no sign of her.

Their Gypsy friends had come to town with a small cart pulled by a pony. From the back of the cart, Grandmother sold roosters and rabbits and apparently was doing a brisk business. Samson had his dog, Jinx, who performed tricks. In payment people tossed coins, mostly pennies, into a copper dish on the ground.

"Lilly!" Samson hurried over but, looking around, seemed to stop himself short of hugging the child. "Would you like to dance with Jinx?" He tied a skirt like a small ruffled apron around the dog's middle and commanded him to dance. The animal stood on his back feet and took careful steps in a circle. Lilly, unable to clap because her hands were full, cried, "Oh, Samson, he's so smart and so cute. Can you teach my kitty tricks?" Grandmother came around the side of the cart holding a large black and white rabbit, the only one left. "And who is this lovely lady?" she asked Samson.

"This is Lilly, Grandmother. She is Martin's sister."

Lilly held her candy between her knees to free a hand for petting the rabbit. The crowd had dispersed so Grandmother and Lilly sat on the open back of the cart and played with the rabbit. Soon Lilly held the large, warm animal in her own lap.

Grandmother smiled. "I am glad this one no sell; she is my favorite."

Martin coaxed Samson far enough from the wagon to
be out of earshot. Trying to keep an anxious tone out of his
voice, he asked, "How's Ruby?"

Samson's laugh rang loud. "She asked me this very morning if I have any news of you."

"She did?"

Samson nodded. Grandmother called to him.

"We must buy our supplies before the mercantile closes,"
Samson explained. "We're staying in town this evening for
Grandmother to do fortunes." As he helped the old woman
off the cart he said, "Grandmother, tell Martin about himself.
He's curious about your second sight."

Grandmother took Martin by the elbow. "Come. You
walk." She steered him back up the street in the direction of
the store. Samson and Lilly followed after tying the dog to
the cart and caging the rabbit.

Martin had to concentrate on shortening his stride to
match that of the tiny woman. Eventually she spoke. "Is not
that I always see special details," she explained. "Sometimes
maybe, yes."

Martin was embarrassed by Samson's request. He'd never
much wondered what his future might be . . . not until he met
Ruby anyway. Since the wedding he'd thought plenty about
seeing her. Feeling slightly foolish, he extended his hand,
palm up, but the small woman merely clasped it in both of
her own.

"I no need to look at lines and wrinkles to know you,"
she said. "I look here and here," she pointed to her eyes and
head, then laid a hand on her heart as if pledging allegiance.
"I see that trials have come to your family."

Martin mentally ticked off the troubles. There was Dan's
death, Meehan wanting to take the farm for taxes, and now
Pa. Ma seemed to be getting better, but she worried constantly that Pa might not fully recover. Martin had dealt with
his concerns by working as hard as he could.

"But you are lucky; you have friends."

Martin thought she referred to the past, to Samson's

weeks of helping him on the farm. "But you need much more. The answer to your problems will reach you if you pay attention to the people you love." She held her hand again over her heart.

Martin didn't know what this meant. He wondered if it had to do with Ruby. He looked down at Grandmother's severe, unsmiling face.

"Is that all?" he asked.

She patted his arm. "Is plenty. You good boy," she said and turned to climb the stairs into Forest's Dry Goods.

Samson waited on the store's steps.

"About Ruby," Martin said. When Sam rolled his eyes at hearing his cousin's name again, Martin assumed his teacher's voice, "We have a saying, 'the squeaky wheel gets the grease.'"

"*We* say the squeaky wheel gets *replaced*. I will talk to her. Can you meet me for fishing tomorrow morning?"

CHAPTER

M artin overslept. It had been late when they returned
from town the night before, and he'd carried the sleeping Lilly into the dark house.

He stood and stretched, making a moaning sound. His
arms still over his head, he turned slowly, wondering why
empty haylofts compelled people to walk in circles. Perhaps
because it felt like a large, empty circus tent. A yawn shook
him to his toes; then he swung his muscular arms down to
his sides.

He peeked out the hayloft door, the best vantage point on
their land. He had been doing this a lot lately, while holding his breath. But now he breathed deeply. The waiting
was over. Not just one or two blades of growth visible only
by squatting on the ground, today there was a green tinge
floating above the soil everywhere. At last the dirt and seeds
verified another of Mr. Perry's lessons: "The smaller the seed,
the faster it germinates." He had done it. He and Sam. The
crops were finally up.

He dressed quickly. Through shafts of dusty sunlight
in the corner stood the trunks where he and Pa had sat and
talked months ago. He walked over and sifted through the
quilt squares, discarded toys, and the crinkly old corset. At
the bottom of one chest lay the set of black buttons. They

were connected through their shanks by a length of knotted gray string.

A passage in Cora's diary described such buttons . . . *jet buttons* she had called them. They were nothing out of the ordinary, but sparkled in a pretty way. He tried to imagine a time when a gift as small as these buttons would have been remarkable. He wrapped the buttons in the quilt squares. He would give them to Lilly.

He went to the house, quilt squares in hand. But his good intentions withered when he saw Ma reading papers spread on the table.

"Good morning, Martin."

"What's all that?" he asked without greeting her.

Ma took a moment to answer. "Mr. Meehan stopped by yesterday afternoon to check some things—storage in the barn, which fields are planted now. Those sorts of things."

Meehan must have seen Martin in town and hightailed it out here. "Why?" he asked.

"So as to be ready if your pa decides to sell. He left these." Martha looked up into her son's face and continued, "He's just being thorough, giving us options. He thinks we'd be lucky to get much for the place. We don't have things as updated here as some folks have."

Martin wanted to tell his mother to believe the opposite of anything Meehan had to say. He had taken charge of so much—moved thousands of pounds of rock off the fields, plowed, harrowed, planted. But none of that mattered if Ma wanted to sell. And Pa would do what Ma wanted, especially if she kept getting better. What did his opinion matter, when, with the stroke of a pen . . .

Martin stormed through the house from back to front, taking half a loaf of bread with him. As he stomped across the porch, Lilly shrank back a step, like a mouse scurrying for cover. Martin stuffed the bread under his elbow in the same way she held her doll, and picked up her hand.

He forced his voice to sound calmer than he felt. "Here,

Lilly, you take these." He didn't manage to sound kind exactly.

She looked at him, bewildered.

"I found them in the barn. A set of nice dress buttons and some old quilt squares. They belonged to . . . ahh, a nice girl like you."

No thanks came. As though he had never given her anything before, Lilly stood staring at the items in her palm.

Martin had to think, had to clear his mind and try to think like Meehan. He grabbed the pail and settled to milk Ella. He pressed his head against her firm side and remembered how once in Stillwater he'd been jostled against a pregnant woman in a crowded train lobby. He was young, and his face was pushed into her belly. He'd expected it to be soft, but it felt just like Ella's flank, tight like the skin on a drum.

He shut his eyes. He hadn't hated the work; he would do it all over again. He *would* do it again next year if he had the chance. If they didn't walk away from this place where his ancestors lay buried. Where Cora was buried. And what about the taxes? Were you put off your place the very next day? Maybe it was possible to pay them late, after the harvest. He would ask about this at the bank if only Meehan weren't the banker.

He pushed away from the cow, upsetting the three-legged stool as he rose. He grabbed the bucket and was about to swing the barn door open when Lilly pulled it from the other side.

"I was just about to call you." Martin thrust the pail into her hand. "Here, take this to the house."

Lilly stood before him, unmoving. In her other hand she held her best Sunday dress. It was brown with ivory piping around the collar. Martin knew the decorative edge was called piping because of the endless hours of sewing discussions he had endured last winter. Just like he knew a thimble was worn on the middle finger of the same hand that holds the needle to control its direction. Lilly had cried about want-ing to protect the fingers underneath the piece of work, the fingers the sharp end sometimes struck, but Aunt Ida held firm.

Lilly had replaced the buttons on the dress bodice, exchanging plain beige buttons with holes for the ornamen-tal black ones that were attached by unseen shanks. She held forward the neatly folded dress. "See what a difference they make! I could add them to the cuffs also, but Aunt Ida says I'll be more likely to rub them off since they stick out."

Martin couldn't be bothered now by a small girl and talk of buttons. Yet he held vivid images in his mind of Cora with these buttons. He took a moment to study Lilly's upturned face.

"Thank you for the buttons," she said in a thin voice.

Martin touched her head, then gently batted a curl that hung fat and springy over her ear. Ma called them sausage curls. He had not felt Lilly's hair in a long time, silky like corn tassels and just as smoothly cool to the touch.

"Who else would I give them to? You're the prettiest girl here." He wondered how it had taken him so long to notice Lilly, to give even the slightest sliver of his attention to her. He had cared more for a girl he would never meet or know except on paper. He thought about Cora, and about Dan, and how short life can be. "I think you should go ahead and put them on the sleeves, too, if you want."

Martin was late getting away. When he first approached the lake, Samson tried to ignore him. But the good-natured boy couldn't pretend to be angry for long.

Martin hurried out onto the familiar log. "Sorry I'm late."

Samson smiled and pulled a stringer of fish out of the water where the boys had first met.

It was a hot, dry day. Martin balanced on the log until he was over deep water, then rested back on a strong branch. He told his friend everything. Everything about Meehan and Ma seeming to believe whatever the man told her.

Sam listened to it all, then said, "I did not know it was this hard to own land."

"It's a gamble the crops will pay—that's what Meehan tells her and that much is true. I could use some insurance to help me keep the place. Remember the story I told you about some treasure on my farm?"

"Your grandparents," Samson nodded.

"And my aunt, their daughter who died at about my age. I didn't tell you something else though. When we moved here I found my aunt's diary in a trunk in the barn." With one hand poised over the other, Martin wrote on his palm in a sign language the boys now performed without thinking—*diary*. What if Sam thought him strange for reading a girl's diary? "I've been reading it. Read the whole thing actually. Read every reference and clue."

Samson pulled in a line that had no fish on it. He coiled the string, then placed it, lasso style, on a broken limb.

"She talks about life on the homestead. She makes it sound so interesting. She talks about a family inheritance. Maybe it's true, or was true long ago. Now my best chance of keeping this place rests on a secret treasure my pa doesn't even believe in. She died young, my Aunt Cora. And fast. She died shortly after writing it."

"What is this treasure?"

"It never says. I mean, I read the whole thing, but she didn't mention what it was. Only that she hid it." Martin shook his head. "I don't think she really understood its value. I've looked everywhere but down the well. I've sifted through the entire homestead and I still don't even know what it is I'm looking for."

"Sifted through?" Samson didn't understand.

"Searched, you know, rummaged through." Martin made busy motions with his hands.

Samson nodded slowly, then reversed the motion and shook his head from side to side. "You must try to figure this out before Mr. Meehan convinces your ma."

"It's strange how little bits of her diary keep floating back to me. They stick in my mind like lines of poetry. But I've never been able to piece out what it is I should be looking for." Martin lifted the stringer of fish. "These are yours today. So, Sam, did you think of a way for me to see Ruby again?"

Samson adjusted his feet on the rotting bark and chose his words carefully. "As my friend, and Grandmother's guest, my people tolerated your presence at the wedding. I'm sorry, Martin, but you would not be seen as a proper suitor for Ruby. We do not even have a word for a *gadje* man marrying a Roma woman. It isn't done."

There it was. Samson disapproved of him for what he was—or at least the rest of his people did. Probably they felt as strongly about him as Aunt Ida did about the Gypsies. "We're just friends is all. What's the harm in seeing her one more time? You said you won't camp here past summer any- way." Martin didn't want to be a suitor exactly, did he? It was just that he had been dreaming of the girl with green eyes and beautiful hair. And didn't Sam's grandmother say to pay attention to those you love in order to find answers? Did he love Ruby? He sure thought so whenever he recalled dancing with her.

"I will try to arrange for you to meet her here tomorrow night at sunset. Don't be late. She likes you, but Ruby changes her mind easily."

The next twenty-four hours passed like three years for Martin. He slept poorly through the night, waking from dreams in which he chased bags of gold or discovered a drawer filled with money.

Ma had neatly tucked away the bank papers. All day Martin concentrated on details from Cora's diary. He had searched thoroughly for a doll's house but, except for the few trunks in the hayloft, none of the original homestead belongings remained. Now he studied the plowshares to be certain they hadn't been crafted in Sweden with a metalsmith's signature on them.

It galled Martin to think that Meehan might get this place and see something he had missed. He squeezed his eyes and remembered the painting of the homestead on Mr. Perry's wall. What other buildings had been here in Cora's lifetime that no longer existed? Martin thought best while working. He cleaned the barn and patched the rail fence in the afternoon, but by day's end he had convinced himself there was no treasure hidden anywhere.

The day was broken up only by the arrival of Mr. Perry, who brought a letter from Pa. Ma was overjoyed to learn he would be ready to make the journey home in just two weeks. Decisions would be made in two weeks.

Martin shivered while he bathed in the kitchen during the evening, while the women and Lilly worked in the garden. He had the patience to add only two large kettles of boiling water from the stove to the tub of cold well water he had carried in with buckets. But it had been such a hot day that he didn't mind the cool soaking. The evening was a repeat of the one before: after supper, he yawned loudly, said good night, and went to the barn while the women prepared their baths. Martin waited in the dark loft for the lanterns from the house to go out. He left through the corral behind the barn, where Finn and Marshall were enjoying the warm evening air. Not wanting to arrive at the lake smelling like a horse, Martin decided to walk. But he walked fast to arrive well in advance of Ruby so there would be no chance she would leave if he wasn't there.

At dusk, Martin saw Sam approaching with Ruby. Despite the dry heat, Ruby wore a lightly woven shawl and scarf. The friends visited briefly; then Samson left to take a walk, telling Ruby, "I'll be nearby. We'll leave in one hour."

Ruby carried a basket that contained a mat, which she spread on the ground. Neither she nor Martin spoke as she set out several dishes of sweets and cheese. With the food to focus on, conversation came easier. Martin considered telling Ruby about Cora's diary. He decided to approach the subject by asking about books.

"We don't read," Ruby said simply. "Only some Gypsy men read. No women. Reading to us means telling fortunes, like my *baba*. Some Roma, my people, don't even speak English. Samson speaks the best English of us, because he listens in towns and sits outside stores and schoolroom windows. He speaks only English to me so I will learn."

Martin was embarrassed. He had assumed she could read. Samson and Ruby indeed came from a different culture. He searched his mind for a safe topic. "Where will you go after this?"

"Probably to marry," Ruby said. "It is late."

"We only just got here." Martin wondered if he had heard her right about getting married.

"No, it is late for me. Most Gypsy girls marry by twelve or thirteen. The girls at the wedding, with their scarves tied behind their heads, they are all married."

Ruby gathered her shawl around her. Her green scarf was tied under her chin. "Do I not speak properly, because of my English?"

Martin saw her mood darken. "No, Ruby, no. It's very interesting—your life. There's so much I don't understand. But it's not your English." His knee brushed hers. Silently they both looked down at their clothes. Ruby fingered a heavy necklace.

"We also wear coins, and much of our jewelry and buttons are made from gold or silver. We Roma keep our valuable things in wearable forms, not in banks or stored away."

"That's interesting." Martin meant it. He carried little of value himself. His everyday pocket contents consisted of a small knife, a half dime from 1854, and the wooden horse Samson had given him. He could spend the half dime, same as a nickel, but he liked carrying it.

Samson had moved down the shore where they could no longer hear him chunking rocks into the water. The evening was very still. Martin lay back and pointed to the darkening sky. As their eyes adapted and twilight deepened, the stars shone more brightly. Soon Ruby was telling him stories and legends her people believed about the heavenly bodies. Martin, who had studied Greek mythology in school, said very little, finding her folktales more interesting than any he knew. He had never studied the stars with a girl before. He pushed everything from his mind, including the time, trusting Sam as Ruby's chaperone to return when necessary. Martin succeeded at shutting out the world until puffs of smoke began to blur his view of the stars.

"Do you smell that?" Ruby asked.

It dawned clear as well water that one of the senses Martin had been ignoring was the smell of something burning. He jumped to his feet. "Fire!" He turned in a half circle, suddenly all senses alert. "That way. Damn. Stay here."

CHAPTER
23

With everything so dry, fire was a constant concern. A swollen black cloud billowed from the earth, the earth near home. The sight took Martin's breath away, just like when Dan died. So this is life: constantly losing the people you love in various terrible ways. He ran flat out. It was almost a mile.

Ruby raced her long legs to keep up. At the road Martin heard, then saw, a running team and wagon. Ruby stepped into the darkness, her arms outstretched to signal the driver to stop. But Martin pushed her across the road out of harm's way. "He'd never see you in time," he shouted, running again. He'd seen Robert Perry lashing his horses as he probably never had before. Martin was glad Mr. Perry hadn't delayed by stopping for them.

He had hoped that the fire was just a tree ignited by lightning. But there was no doubt now that it was a building and the fire was at his place. His lungs burned but his feet wouldn't slow. Ruby fell behind when she tired.

Martin saw the two tall horses, backlit by the glow of blazing buildings. They paced, well away from the downed pasture fence, which had been flattened by the beasts whose usual gentle nature tolerated being corralled. He looked around the farmyard, taking in the scene in an instant.

Everything was burning. Right through the space where the barn roof once stood he could see the house, illuminating the night with bright fire.

"Ma! Lilly! Auntie!"

Martin didn't make decisions so much as he ignored things. He ignored the barn and the death calls of a lone cow. The well? No time. On his way to the burning house he ran through the side yard, tearing sheets from the clothesline, yelling their names. The main door to the house was engulfed. The roof blazed. He flew to the garden door; it writhed with fire also.

Darkness and smoke made it impossible to see anything but the flames themselves. They had to be inside. If they'd gotten out, they would have answered him. "Ma! Lilly! Auntie!" He kept screaming, but the fire sucked the sound away. He put up his arm to protect his eyes from the waves of heat.

There was no back door, but he raced to the back of the house anyway. How could it take so long to get around the tiny house? Back here smoke poured out of the single window, but flames had not reached it yet. Martin saw Sam's back as the boy jumped and jumped again, finally getting a handhold on the sill and pulling himself up. Coughing, Sam struggled to balance, half in and half out. Martin ran up and boosted his friend over the windowsill into the burning house. He heard no screaming or shouting. Just the loud, living fire. Flames began to unfurl around the window frame and to emerge between the siding boards. Using the sheets, Martin swatted wildly at the flames leaping up the dry, unpainted siding. How would Sam find anyone in the dark when he'd never even been in the house before? Martin tried to jump up onto the high sill as Sam had done.

Lilly swirled into sight at the window. Martin raised his arms to grab her—then his aunt too, as light as his sister. Now Mr. Perry was there, taking Aunt Ida from Martin's arms and carrying her away. Sam appeared in the opening with a smoldering rug over his shoulders and head. He lowered Ma, feet first, to Martin. Then Sam tumbled out.

They moved as a huddled mass through the garden toward the drive. Mr. Perry had stopped well back from the billowing fire. His horses champed and stomped.

"They smell death," Samson choked. "The cow, I am sorry. I only had time to go into the house."

Martin knew that somewhere inside he would feel sorry about Ella's death, if ever he could feel again. But right now he couldn't feel anything, not even his blistered fingers or stinging eyes. Everyone was safe; he could think of nothing else.

Ruby caught up and spoke quietly with Samson, then disappeared down the road. Lilly shook as if cold. Martin picked her up and held her. They had nothing to wrap her in, not a jacket or a blanket. Ma, Aunt Ida, and Lilly climbed onto Mr. Perry's wagon seat, Ma's arms around the others. Mr. Perry offered to take the women to his house, but Ma refused, saying she couldn't leave yet. There was something about the fire that demanded watching to the finish. Martin and Mr. Perry rested on the ground, leaning against wagon wheels. Martin had felt this useless only once before, on the day Dan died. The siding burned away to reveal the original log structure underneath; then that was consumed too.

At first light it was clear there was nothing left to burn, that it was the dirt itself that still smoked. The trees that surrounded the house were half black, half green. The barn was such a melted wreckage that it was difficult to see where Ella had stood and died. The large horses kept their distance below the pasture, somewhat settled now by the familiarity of dawn and Samson, who sat with them through the night.

Aunt Ida sucked her teeth and said defeatedly, "Everything's gone, Martha."

Ma stood up in Mr. Perry's wagon, waking Lilly, whose head had rested in her lap. Ma spread her blackened hands and arms to take in the devastation before them.

"What everything?"

Mr. Perry stood. Martin stood too, nervously uncertain

just which Ma—the improving Ma or the Ma of this past
year—was going to speak.

"We hated that little house, and yes it's gone. But my children aren't! The barn is a loss, and I'm sorry about Ella. But a
cow can be replaced. The garden is planted, and thank God it
wasn't up yet to catch fire. We didn't even have a scarecrow
out to burn. It's a farm, Aunt Ida." Ma of the outstretched
arms turned from right to left on her wagon pulpit. "And it's
still here! Look. It isn't all gone. It's just starting."

Everyone looked where her filthy hands invited. Beyond
the charred sticks that grew up from yesterday's foundations
lay the fields. A green fringe covered them, lightly, like mist.
Martin was unprepared for his feelings, both of loss and of
joy that so much was growing. He had to find Sam, be sure
Sam saw it. He remembered Sam saying—it felt so long ago—
Land is hopes.

Full light found the friends below the barn, taking stock of
the damage. The fire's own din had commanded silence, and
in its confusion no one had asked yet who Samson was. Both
boys' eyes were pink ovals in blackened faces. Martin's voice
was cracked from hacking and screaming. He surveyed his
entire home and barn, reduced to nothing. "What did I do?
Did I leave a lantern lit? Did Meehan torch the barn?"

Sam wrapped an arm around his shoulder. "No. I don't
think so. Maybe it was lightning. The barn was on fire first.
It is bigger," he said, raising one hand above the other, "taller
than the house, and sparks showered down."

"Thank God you got here when you did, Sam. Thank God
you got my family out." While thinking of all he was grateful
for, Martin winced at the thought that Pa could have lost his
family a second time here.

A great commotion rose from the direction of Mr. Perry's wagon. Standing in the wagon, Aunt Ida pointed and
screamed where the road turned into the farm. The boys
came running.

"Here they come! The murderers, they burned us out."
Aunt Ida's finger looked a foot long as she pointed down the
access road. "Gypsies are coming."

The boys raced up. Mr. Perry, unable to cope with a hys-
terically screaming woman, stood between the heads of his
two hitched horses.

"Where's Lilly?" his aunt shouted.

Martin jumped onto the wagon and grabbed her arm. She
was thin yet surprisingly hard like a chair rung.

"I don't know where Lilly is, but she's fine. These people
who are coming are my friends."

Aunt Ida went stiff. "They live in Gypsy wagons like that
photography fellow? Regular folks wouldn't do that."

"They live in wagons, Auntie, because they *are* Gypsies."
Martin turned her face from the road to look at him. "And
this is Sam. Samson. He's Roma too."

Samson looked down at the dirt.

"But all that matters is that he's a friend. And he saved
your life last night."

Aunt Ida looked shocked.

Ma looked from boy to boy. "Yes, Martin, what *was* he
doing here in the first place?"

"He's my friend, Ma. I could never have done all the work
this spring without him. Sam helped me every day with rocks
and plowing and planting."

Martin could tell his mother was still confused. "I was
gone last night, Ma, and Sam knew it. I wasn't in the barn.
If he hadn't come here . . ." He turned to Sam. "Why did you
come?"

"To see Finn and Marshall."

"Gone where?" Ma asked Martin.

Mr. Perry walked up to Ma. "I can vouch for the boy,
ma'am." He gestured to Sam. "This here's a fine boy. He can
work for me for as long as he cares to stay."

While the group sorted out Samson's identity, two beautiful wooden caravan wagons pulled up, drawn by matched

sets of horses. Ruby managed one wagon while Sam's grandmother sat on the front seat of another next to a driver. Aunt Ida, soot-faced and speechless, looked upon their arrival as a fate worse than the fire.

Martin was glad to have the diversion so he didn't have to answer his mother's last question about where he'd gone last night. From her wagon seat, Grandmother smiled infectiously on them all. She had the kindest smile Martin knew, one that did not seem out of place in the face of such hardship.

Grandmother got down and put her hand through Samson's arm. "You help me speak, yes?" She turned to Martha. "You are Martin's mother, yes? Your Martin is a special friend to us. Once, in the spring, he save my Samson from drowning. He's been our true friend, something he must have learned from you."

She released Samson's arm and touched Martin's filthy face. "I have been waiting to help you." She gestured toward the caravan Ruby occupied. "For you. This we give you to live in. It is a full home, no? You take. Come see."

Grandmother's eyes challenged Aunt Ida to get down. For a moment Martin thought she wouldn't budge, but curiosity appeared to get the better of her. Grandmother walked to the back door and threw it open. She petted a goat tied to the wagon.

"This is for milking. And this is for living." She climbed three stairs and demonstrated all the comforts of the miniature house on wheels. Grinning at Martin she explained, "We had a wedding. Two people became one and only need one home. This we do not need for now. We leave until another year."

Grandmother and Ruby set a table and chairs outside by the garden's edge and efficiently organized a meal. In Grandmother's wagon they cooked eggs and coffee that they served with sweetened bread and butter. Even shy Mr. Perry ate.

CHAPTER

News of the disaster reached town, and by afternoon three wagons of people had arrived to assess the fire and offer help. Happy to stay on the edge of the crowd, Martin was the first to hear the clickety-click of Mr. Meehan's car pull off the road and climb toward the farmyard.

Martin had no barn to turn into, so he stood waiting for Meehan to pull the automobile to a stop. "Morning," the man said, clutching the thin steering wheel.

Martin didn't answer. It certainly wasn't any kind of a good morning.

"How's your family doing? I heard about last night. Did everyone make out fine in the fire?"

"All but the cow."

"And the buildings, of course," Meehan added. "It would have been best if you folks had sold to me before this happened. Affects the value."

The weeks of intense work had hardened Martin like hickory. He looked down at the man on the seat. "As you can see, we're still here."

"And your pa is still behind on payments. I've been too kindhearted to put out a family that has fallen on hard times."

The chances of harvesting the fields and getting moved

into a permanent structure before hard winter did look impossible. But at least they had survived. So had Finn and Marshall. True, they had no money, but they had friends. Friends were something Meehan would never understand. Mr. Perry would loan his cultivator, harvester, and other implements without even being asked. And Sam and his grandmother had already provided a home that would serve a good five months until winter. By then Martin could at least build a sauna building. He still had plenty of trees and could borrow an ax and saw. Many Scandinavian immigrants had spent their first winter or two living in the structure that would later be the family's sauna building for bathing, which was built large enough to have two rooms—one for changing and the other for the woodstove to heat water. Martin would make it maybe twelve by fourteen feet. They could spend a winter in that. They'd be cramped but warm.

"You don't even have a wagon. With no home, no barn, and no harvesting equipment, you'll be out of here in a month."

Martin leaned over the door until Meehan recoiled from the rancid smell of Martin's clothes. "Maybe so," Martin said. "Like you say, we're poor all right, but don't you ever come near this farm again."

By late afternoon Ma, Lilly, Aunt Ida, and Martin had bathed in the caravan wagon and changed into clean clothes brought out by the townspeople.

Before Samson's grandmother left with her driver and the horses that had pulled the spare wagon, she instructed Samson in Romany.

"My grandmother says to tell you 'Every disaster courts opportunity.'"

Martin couldn't wrap his exhausted mind around a riddle. "I don't know what that's supposed to mean."

Grandmother let go of Sam and embraced Martin, smiling, while she struggled to find her own words. She squeezed his arm four times, once for each word she spoke, *"From bad comes good.* Remember the things I have told you; look to the ones you love for answers."

Later, while Ma and Aunt Ida napped, Samson sat with Martin on chairs at the garden's edge. A brightly colored fabric flashed under the largest pine at the end of the garden.

"There's Lilly, playing with her dolls," Samson observed, exhausted from his nightlong vigil and long day.

Martin stood and stretched. "I haven't seen her since

breakfast." He left his friend and walked to her through the planted rows that would become beans and carrots.

Lilly sat with her back to a tree trunk from which huge roots radiated across the top of the soil. She sat in the V between two large roots. One root over, her doll was tucked under a quilt. Little things were placed all around the tree as if each space between roots were a room.

"How did you have time to save Stella in the fire?" Martin asked, stooping down before her. He had never knelt down to Lilly's height before, only just looked down at her.

"She was here. She always sleeps out here in dry weather. This is her room." Lilly indicated the triangle of pine needles between two tree roots.

He fingered Stella's blanket. "Did you make this from those squares I gave you?"

Lilly nodded. She turned to her other side and indicated a setting of dishes. "This is my parlor; you can come in. It's cool here."

Martin sat between two large roots and looked out at the fire-flattened hilltop. The pines were old; their bottom branches, eight feet from the ground, created a natural roof under which to play. He imagined Lilly had spent much time here all spring, but he'd never noticed. It was indeed the coolest place on the site, and he realized the caravan should be placed here in the shade. He stood to get Finn and Marshall to pull it.

Martin walked back through the garden, away from Lilly's little playhouse in the trees. Snippets of Cora's diary tried to come to him through his weary mind.

we played in my doll's house to escape the sun

we took a nap in the shade of my doll's house

the dowry, which I hid safely in my doll's house

Martin spun on his heel and studied the care with which Lilly had created a perfect little house, a doll's house. His neck went cold at the realization that another girl had played on this hill in a doll's house, a doll's house no one could find.

But it couldn't have been. According to the homestead picture at Mr. Perry's, these five trees had been tiny when Cora was a child, the height of bushes—too small to sit under. He shook his head and walked toward the smoldering house.

Martin passed his chopping stump and wondered about the many lives of this tree. He pictured it as the tall elm it had been in the painting that hung at Mr. Perry's. How lush and full it was when his grandparents built in its shade. Eventually it had died but remained for years as a handy chopping stump, the rest becoming fuel or maybe furniture. Now the stump was charred and strewn with debris. But this tree that both he and Aunt Cora knew—each in their own way—had once been the centerpiece of the yard.

He studied its huge dead roots, roots he had steadied his foot on hundreds of times to swing the ax. He imagined a young girl playing under the tree, and through the imagining felt for the first time as if he saw things clearly. Martin turned on his heel and ran to the garden.

Aunt Ida's spade stood there, filthy with ash but usable. He ran back to the stump and went to work digging. When he'd finished in one area, he stepped over the root and dug in the next space.

"What are you doing?"

"Digging. Digging under the whole stump," Martin said to Samson. It seemed an adequate explanation between friends. Samson retrieved the steel rod, which had survived underneath the stone boat away from the barn. Silently, Samson placed it under the rotted root where Martin was digging and bore his weight down on the end. They needed an ax to sever the roots at the soil line, but all of the tools had burned. Martin thought about that, about each of his grandfather's woodworking tools melting to nothing in the fire, actually fueling the fire with their ancient wooden handles. One by one Martin beat the roots with the spade as Samson bore down on the pry bar. They found the backbone to dig a while more. Every time he heard the scrape of the spade against a buried rock Martin poked around, dislodging baseball-size stones from the tangled roots.

Long after sweat made muddy streaks down their filthy faces and necks, the spade struck something with a dull but solid thud. For the first time the object he hit didn't sound like a rock. Martin fell to his knees and scooped cool dirt with his hands. He reached deep into the hole as Sam kept levering back on the pole that supported the stump just enough so Martin could work under it.

Thirty minutes after they began, with breaks only long enough to reposition themselves, Martin dragged a small wooden box from the ground. The soot- and soil-blackened boys exchanged questioning glances.

Martin sat down on the earth, breathing hard, and brushed off the box. Samson abandoned the prying pole and sat with him. For a minute Martin just held the box.

"It reminds me of a tiny coffin," Martin said. "My pa taught me how to make coffins watertight." He turned the box in his hands. "Pa says a carpenter can make just about anything once he masters a cradle and a coffin." The lid was swollen in place. He turned it on its side and struck it with the only tool available to him, but the spade did nothing to spring it free. He fished for his pocketknife and pried the blade into a seam at the top of the box. It reluctantly squeaked free, reminding him of the sound that stones made when he forced them from their sod moorings.

The box was stuffed with oilskin. Martin tipped the heavy bundle into his hand, then slowly unwrapped the fabric, which had been bound and tied with a leather strip. He looked at Samson.

The boy just shrugged.

The next layer, a piece of muslin, fell limply in pieces to the ground. Left in his hand was a roll of more tightly woven fabric. It had once been white, and it looked lightweight but was deceptively heavy. Martin unrolled it.

Samson looked bewildered. "What is that?"

Martin had already figured that Gypsy women with their loose clothes probably didn't wear these, so he explained, "It's a corset." He unwrapped it completely and held it expanded as a circle in front of his chest.

Samson nodded in understanding.

"Mighty heavy though." Martin couldn't imagine a woman wearing something like this, especially in hot weather.

Mother says she kept it with her every day of the long journey.

Martin laid the corset facedown on his lap. He counted twelve casings, each formed by two seams sewn close together. He pulled two rigid stays out of their casings and studied them. Often when Ma and Aunt Ida washed corsets they left the stays standing in a glass on the windowsill. He had played with them as a child. The ones he remembered had been light and slightly bendable. These were as rigid as steel. Yet they were fashioned for comfort, smooth and rounded at the ends.

About the size of flat pencils, these felt heavier than iron. Martin handed one to Sam and brought one up to his face for closer scrutiny. He could barely make out near the tip the familiar shield that had been his great-grandfather's metal-smith signature in Sweden: crown and sword.

The handcrafted sticks of metal with their tiny crowns and swords like lightning bolts glowed bronze in the afternoon sun.

The boys rested, passing the similar yet unique rods back and forth for inspection.

"I don't know what I am holding, Sam," Martin said, still

exhausted and awestruck by the discovery, "but what if this means I can pay you now for all your hard work?"

Sam looked as horrified as the day he realized that rock-clearing was not a onetime job. He held up both hands. "I did not work for money, for to be paid. I work for friendship."

"Not money then. Take one of these."

Sam shook his head at the offered stay.

"Take it because my great-grandfather made it." Martin dug in the pocket of his filthy pants, felt again the knife, the half dime, and pulled out the horse. "You once asked me to accept something made by your grandfather." He held both palms open, a horse in one, a slice of metal in the other.

Sam chose.

CHAPTER

After sharing the discovery with Ma, Aunt Ida, and Lilly, he and Sam returned the treasure to the only place of safekeeping left on the farm, the earth. He told the women about the diary. It soothed his guilt over losing it to the fire and never being able to share it with Pa or with the one it really belonged to—Lilly. He thanked Lilly with an afternoon of endless twirling.

The food and clothing that people brought helped them get through their first night after the fire, and the gypsy wagon was comfortable shelter. The women and Lilly slept in the traveling home; Martin slept outside. The fire could have been much worse. It could have been harvesttime with fields of tall, swaying wheat and field corn on stalks so dry they rustled. The fire could have coursed across the county.

Martin woke up realizing that the real loss from the fire was yet to come. After breakfast he walked out on the land until all he could smell was fresh air.

Sam found him standing on one of their irregular rock piles between fields. They stood a while, inspecting all they'd done together, the silence between them not comfortable this time. They shifted from foot to foot to maintain balance. A hawk with broad wings appeared to be napping in the sky above them. Wildflowers that covered the berms between fields looked like fancy stitchwork connecting quilt squares. Martin glimpsed Sam out of the corner of his eye, and that moment confirmed his suspicions that Sam's people would pull up stakes, afraid to remain in the vicinity of a fire they might be blamed for. He went back to studying the turned and planted earth. He hoped that when he found his voice, the words wouldn't be what he'd just been thinking: *I owe you everything.* "When do you go?"

"We are ready."

"Won't you stay for the harvest, Sam?"

Silence.

"Cut some wheat, put up hay? Miss all that fun?" *You are the best friend I ever had.*

"I have to go with them."

"My whole family wants you to stay. I can almost guarantee my aunt won't shoot you. And my pa—." He was going to say *My pa needs to meet you* and *You know Mr. Perry would keep you on.* But Martin knew the truth—his time with this uncommon boy was over—and he could have mouthed it with Sam when he simply said, "Grandmother needs me."

Sam looked at the boulders they were balancing on. "I will return someday to your rock farm."

"I will always be here."

That afternoon Martin took one of the stays from its resting place. Riding Finn bareback into town was like sitting on a bouncing tabletop. As he jogged along, Martin made a plan to finish knocking down the buildings and bury some of the debris to remove the scorched smell and memories. This time, though, he'd be doing the work alone.

At Olsson's Clocks, Watches & Fine Jewelry, Mr. Olsson introduced himself as the manager. The elderly man looked kind but lost his smile when Martin told him his name. Mr. Olsson stared for such a long moment that Martin worried he might be a comrade of Meehan's. Or maybe he had missed a spot. Every time they touched anything their hands and faces got dirty again.

"Sir?" Martin broke the silence.

Mr. Olsson shook his head slowly from side to side. "Martin Gunnarsson," he finally repeated. "I'm embarrassed, you see. I've meant to come out and meet your family, and now I've heard of the fire and, well, I wish I had."

Martin took the bundle from the pocket of his clean donated pants.

"I must tell you, young man, that seeing you fairly takes away my breath." He put a hand to his heart as if to pledge allegiance. "I knew your Grandpa Gunnarsson long ago. We were contemporaries. We went to war together. You are his likeness." He shook his head again. "I knew Jacob growing up, of course, but you are even more Carl's likeness. Sometimes things skip a generation."

He held out his hand, formally, although they'd already introduced themselves. "It's a pleasure to meet you."

"Thank you, sir. Sometime I'd like to hear more about my grandfather if you don't mind."

"I'd like that too, any time at all. How can I help you today?"

Martin unwrapped the long thin bar of metal. "Can you please tell me what kind of metal this is?"

Mr. Olsson studied it, then carried it to the window where he repeated the inspection with a jeweler's loupe squeezed over one eye. "Where did you get this?"

"It was handed down from my grandmother's father," Martin answered carefully. "Is it copper?"

"No." He studied it like it was a rare gem, like he'd studied Martin only moments before. Treating it like a fragile egg, Mr. Olsson hefted it in one hand to get a sense of its weight.

"Then is it brass?"

"No . . ." Mr. Olsson's voice trailed off.

Martin felt foolish. Thank God he hadn't brought all twelve—no, eleven now. He pressed a palm against the horse in his pocket. He hoped he wouldn't have to explain that he was asking for an appraisal of corset stays. "Is it valuable at all?"

"Oh, yes," the man whispered, intent on inspecting the piece. "Very." He lifted his head, popped the loupe off his eye, and turned to Martin. "This looks to be a very pure bar of gold."

"But it's dark, not yellow."

"This grade of gold is too pure to make jewelry from. It's softer than jewelry-grade gold. Other metal alloys are added to gold to make it stronger, so it will hold up as a ring or a watchcase, and those other metals change its color too."

Mr. Olsson carefully wrapped the piece in clean, soft paper and handed it back to Martin. "Where did you say this came from?"

Martin thought about Cora, then about his grandmother wearing the uncomfortable corset on her overseas journey. He smelled the destroyed homestead on himself despite the borrowed clothes and shuddered at how close he'd come to losing this treasure forever.

"From my ancestors. It's been in the family a long time."

The family of Leonard and Elizabeth Koehnen.

AUTHOR'S NOTE

Fiction is woven of fact, history, and hard work. Then *what if* sparks fly and fire the imagination.

Parts of this story were inspired by true events. My great-aunt, Annie Koehnen, whose parents were Dutch and German, died in Minnesota of diphtheria in 1893. She was eight years old. I grew up in St. Paul with this photograph hanging in our living room. The pencil sketch in the center of the photograph is of Annie, who died before the youngest child, my grandmother, was born. Grandma Minnie sits in the front, wearing a white dress. I grew up thankful for immunizations that protected me from serious contagious disease. But I was curious about those past diseases, too, and often look for epidemic deaths in pioneer graveyards where the single word *cholera* or *diphtheria* may appear on headstones. Sometimes entire families are recorded as dying in a single week or even one day. It made me wonder: *What if* you were the only child left? *What if* you were a helpless baby?

Grandma Minnie was born in 1896 and lived 101 years. She told many stories about the Gypsies who came through their farm community in Minnesota. Throughout her life she spoke of her fear of them, and like Aunt Ida in this story, Grandma believed they would steal children, food, clothing, and equipment. But *what if* you actually got to know one of those Gypsy kids?

Life expectancy for Americans in 1903 was forty-nine years. Children still commonly died from diphtheria, typhoid, cholera, and measles, which decreased the average life expectancy because many people did not live to adulthood. There were no antibiotics yet to fight scarlet fever or infection. Any wound was treated seriously, as it could lead to blood poisoning. Twenty years after Martin's story, President Calvin Coolidge's sixteen-year-old son died from an infected blister on his toe.

My grandma married a Swedish man, Carl Palmer. Grandpa's brother Martin was fourteen in 1903, like Martin Gunnarsson. My Swedish ancestors did not come to America with a treasure that I know of, although early immigrants commonly brought ironworks such as nails, hinges, and ax heads.

In my living room hangs a rustic oil painting of the Palmer homestead near Bernadotte, Minnesota, dated 1903. Large trees in this painting remind me of the elms on the boulevards in St. Paul where I grew up. As a child I played at the base of those trees, pretending each space between the large roots was a room.

In history, I like the decade from 1900 to 1910. I think of it as a quiet time. Much is written about the years between 1910 and 1920 because of the First World War, and the Roaring Twenties after that, then the Depression of the thirties. During that first decade of the twentieth century, President Theodore Roosevelt governed a country of eighty million people, compared to 319 million citizens today. Farmers (and Gypsies, too) still mostly used horses, although there were some automobiles—about eight thousand throughout the country. While Henry Ford was busy organizing the Ford Motor Company, prosperous farmers might have owned a light team of horses for pulling a wagon or buggy and a heavy team for plowing and logging. Some farmers could also afford to keep saddle horses.

Baseball was big in Martin's day. The first World Series (a best-of-nine series) was played in 1903, with the Boston

Americans winning five games to three over the Pittsburgh Pirates. In this book, Martin helped Samson read English from an actual newspaper report about baseball that spring. That same year Orville and Wilbur Wright made aviation history with their first flight at Kitty Hawk, North Carolina.

Few social or government programs were available at that time to help families in need. If parents could not feed their children, the children were often sent, as Mr. Meehan was as a child, to "work out," usually on a farm where they labored in exchange for food. My father, Robert O'Brien, was sent to work out as a youth on his uncle's horse ranch near Hardin, Montana. He remembered that the Gypsy caravans in eastern Montana during the 1920s still used horses, but trucks were becoming popular. Dad was often asked to turn out restless horses in the morning—ride them fast down the road and back. He entered their stalls holding a stick across his chest, just wider than his body, as the horses sometimes tried to crush him against the wall. I borrowed this detail for Martin in the story.

It is likely that Martin's grandfather volunteered to serve in the Civil War. Minnesota was the first among the states in which no battles were fought to offer troops to President Lincoln. Twenty-four thousand Minnesotans served, half the eligible population of the state. "Minnesota, as a fledgling state, contributed disproportionately to the war through the commitments of its citizens and the valor of its soldiers," states the Minnesota Historical Society's website, where you can read more about the contributions of the thirty-second state.

Many nations of the world have nomadic people known by various names as Gypsies, rovers, walking people, and travelers. Gypsies came to America in the second half of the nineteenth century, when many Europeans immigrated. Aunt Ida incorrectly calls them "heathen Egyptians" because the name *Gypsy* comes from a mistaken belief that their ancestors were from Egypt. In fact, Gypsies came from northwestern India. They call themselves Roma, and the many dialects of the Romany language contain words clearly derived from Indian Sanskrit.

The Roma follow extremely strict guidelines about cleanliness. Ruby would indeed have been shocked to see Martin—a *gadjo* (non-Gypsy)—in their wagon, as his presence would require them to conduct a rigorous cleaning. The Roma are self-governing, and one of the most dreaded punishments a *vitsa* (clan) member can receive is loss of commensality—no longer being accepted at table. The Roma love to feast together, and it would have been bad manners for Martin to decline Samson's grandmother's invitation to stay for dinner. I did take some literary license with the story; for example, in Roma society men and women stay separate at social functions, and Martin would not likely have been dancing with Ruby.

Traditionally the Roma worked as metalsmiths, musicians (their music has influenced great composers, including Haydn, Beethoven, Brahms, and Dvořák), horse dealers, and fortune-tellers. Municipal ordinances against fortune-telling severely curtailed their incomes.

In Martin's time, newspaper reports of Gypsies were usually published to warn people of their presence in an area. They were thought to overcharge and swindle *gadje*. Farm journals from many agricultural areas throughout the country include passages about Gypsies stealing medicine, small animals, implements, and, as Aunt Ida warns, "the clothes off the line." They probably did not have the habit of knocking on a door, and their culture allowed for different methods of distributing wealth. They were consistently feared and often sent packing. Yet it was widely understood that they did not steal from households that provided for them, and many settlers' journals list donations to Gypsies of woven cloth, chickens, and bread. Their wandering lifestyle has historically made census statistics contradictory and unreliable. In many areas of the world, Gypsies have been persecuted. During the Holocaust of the 1930s and 1940s, many Roma in Europe were killed, but counts of how many vary by as much as half a million, due to the undocumented nature of their lifestyle.

The Roma traveled freely throughout the United States and Canada during the late 1800s and the first half of the twentieth century. These accounts from the *Red Wing Daily Republican* describe the visits of Gypsies to this area:

> A number of gypsies who have been in camp near this place for the past few days, canvassed the city yesterday, begging money and making themselves a nuisance generally. Some of the merchants say that it required close watching to keep them from carrying away articles in their spacious pockets or bundles which they carried with them. A trained bear and monkey, and the singing of antiquated songs by young girls, were some of the methods used to attract attention and draw pennies from the pockets of our citizens. (August 15, 1895)

> The gypsies who came to town yesterday were the toughest and dirtiest set of people that ever visited this vicinity. The girls that were supposed to be telling fortunes were "fakes." (October 21, 1898)

> About a week ago a gang of gypsies visited this city. The women told "fortunes" and took many a dollar from our business men. They also visited Pine City, Minnesota, and worked their schemes there. A special to a St. Paul paper says: "There was considerable excitement in this village yesterday over the presence of a gang of bold, bad gypsy women, who pretended to tell fortunes and do tricks requiring coins, which they immediately proceeded to appropriate. Six of them were rounded up last evening and spent the night in the cooler." (October 27, 1898)

Red Wing is the county seat of Goodhue County, and I chose Goodhue County as the setting for *The Search for the Homestead Treasure* because of its unique blend of beautiful farmland, forests, and steep river bluffs that are home to

rattlesnakes. Of the seventeen varieties of snakes found in
Minnesota, only two are poisonous, the timber rattlesnake
and the eastern massasauga. The timber rattlesnake is
found in Goodhue County—and in much greater numbers
in Martin's time than today. In the late 1800s and early
1900s, rattlesnake kills were listed in the county newspapers,
including the length of the snake in feet and inches and the
number of its rattles. Bounties were offered for killing these
snakes until 1989, and five thousand bounties were paid in
1970 alone. By 1984 the timber rattlesnake was designated
a species of concern and in 1996 was reclassified as threat-
ened. Today this species is considered secretive but not
aggressive; a few bites are reported annually in Minnesota,
but there have been no reported deaths from this snake in
the last hundred years.

Much of the rich farmland of Goodhue County was
purchased before the Homestead Act of 1862. Through this
act the government gave 160 acres of untamed land free to
anyone willing to farm it. In order to own a homestead, farmers had to "prove up" their claim, which meant living on the
land for five years and growing crops on a portion of it. The
program was wildly popular and helped to settle our country. But in the short span of forty years, speculators bought
up many family farms, grouped them into larger parcels,
and sold them. By 1900, nine of every ten homesteads were
owned by these land monopolists, banks, or the railroads.

What Martin's family did in leaving town for farming was
very unusual. After 1900, the growing cities were the place to
be! Suddenly there were buyers for farms, and families who
were tired of uncertain weather and all the hard work that
farming required were tempted to sell. But folks who hung
on would have an easier time in the decades to come. Those
with a tie to the land would more readily have food during
the World Wars and the Depression of the 1930s. *What if* we
look ahead twenty-five years and imagine the Gunnarsson
homestead and Martin's family then . . .

ACKNOWLEDGMENTS

My first thanks go to my husband, Kevin, and children, Carolyn and John, for their support and for loving history as I do.

I received help and answers to many questions from Afton Esson, archives and library manager of the Goodhue County Historical Society. Many people have encouraged my writing career, including my sisters, Mary Caskey and Rose Boll, and my friends Mary W. Zbaracki, Jane Hovland, and Mary Treacy O'Keefe. Fellow writers (and one son-in-law) who read and commented on sections or complete drafts include Helen Hemphill, Margi Preus, Bridget Reistad, Linda Glaser, Ann Horowitz, Yvonne Pearson, Naomi Musch, Konnie LeMay, Gwenyth Swain, Anthony Bramante, and Katharine Johnson. Special thanks to Katharine and Dale Johnson for introducing me to the historic Eli Wirtanen homestead, established in 1904.

A vitally important person to this book has been Erik Anderson, University of Minnesota editor and believer in Martin. Thank you for championing this story.

Finally, I'd like to gratefully acknowledge managing editor Laura Westlund for her careful reading and enthusiasm for this story.

Ann Treacy is a freelance writer and children's author. Her writing has been published in *Lake Superior Magazine* and *Highlights for Children* magazine, and she is coeditor, with Margi Preus, of *A Book of Grace*. She lives in Duluth, Minnesota.